MW01058154

When Jordan didn't answer she turned to find out why. She followed his mesmerized gaze to her open suitcase. A lacy pink satin nightgown lay on top.

He stood perfectly still as visions of Macy wearing this garment danced through his head. Thoroughly embarrassed, she quickly grabbed the garment and stuffed it into the drawer.

"Sorry," she said shyly.

"No need to apologize. Seeing that just brought forth images that I have been trying to restrain."

"What types of images?" *Stupid, stupid question, Macy.*

"I imagined us on that big bed, you wearing only that nightgown, me wearing nothing. Our bodies coming together, entwining until we become one. Our pleasure producing a symphony of moans and indistinguishable murmurs of delight. Me kissing you all over and you whimpering my name. Oh Bella, you can see it too, can't you?" Standing in the doorway with his eyes half closed he allowed the images to be permanently implanted in his memory. Macy, overwhelmed, took the only route she knew. Defense.

OBJECT OF HIS DESIRE

A.C. ARTHUR

Genesis Press Inc.

Indigo Love Stories

An imprint Genesis Press Publishing

Genesis Press, Inc.
1213 Hwy 45 North
Columbus, MS 39705

All rights reserved. Except for use in any review, the reproduction
or utilization of this work in whole or in part in any form by any
electronic, mechanical, or other means, not known or hereafter
invented, including xerography, photocopying and recording, or in
any information storage or retrieval system, is forbidden without
written permission of the publisher, Genesis Press, Inc. For information write Genesis Press, Inc., 1213 Hwy 45 North, Columbus,
MS 39705.

All characters in this book have no existence outside the imagination of the author and have no relation whatsoever to anyone bear-
ing the same name or names. They are not even distantly inspired
by any individual known or unknown to the author and all incidents
are pure invention

Copyright© 2003 by A.C. Arthur

ISBN: 1-58571-094-6
Manufactured in the United States of America

First Edition

Visit us at www.genesis-press.com
or call at 1-888-Indigo-1

CHAPTER ONE

The George F. Glenn Hall was decorated in gold and white crepe paper streamers, and iridescent balloons clung to the ceiling. Chandeliers, polished to perfection, sparkled in the candlelight and the hardwood floors gleamed from hours of buffing. Macy swore she could see herself in the brass statue that sat atop the mahogany railing gracing the winding staircase. Descending the stairs slowly she continued to admire the festive atmosphere in the charmingly decorated room. Named for her father's many contributions to Chester County, this hall was a special place to Macy. It symbolized not only what a great man her father was, but what he had achieved in his life. She was extremely proud.

At the bottom of the stairs she could hear the music coming from the ballroom. People were beginning to arrive in steady streams. Macy sighed at the thought of the long night she had ahead of her.

"Excuse me, madam. May I take your wrap?" a tall thin gentleman in a black tuxedo asked her politely.

"Oh! Of course." Macy handed him the chiffon wrap that matched her gown. The look on the man's face assured her that she had chosen the right dress for the occasion. The candy apple-colored material ended dramatically with an asymmetrical hem that shimmered at her knees with rhinestones. In the same rhinestone material two straps clasped at the nape of her neck held the dress in place. However, her ample breasts would have done the job quite nicely on their own. Red nylon stockings with a slight hint of gold glitter gave a shimmering luminescence to her legs. Her jewelry was simple: one gold bangle hung from her right wrist and gold teardrops fell from her earlobes.

She wore very little makeup; her honey-brown skin was naturally flawless. High cheekbones highlighted warm brown eyes and accompanied full lips that were coated with the barest whisper of red gloss.

Macy had always thought she had a quiet beauty so she tended to keep her clothes low key. But tonight she'd felt adventurous and opted to spice up her normal appearance.

She stood in the front entrance occasionally waving to co-workers or clients before gracefully making her way across the room. She felt absolutely giddy with the excitement that bubbled around her. She loved parties and the Women and Children's Charity Ball was the party of the year for the firm.

New York's finest had come out in full force, their five thousand dollar donations having secured entrance into the ball. Before crossing the room she had conversed with the mayor and two other congressmen that had served in Washington with her father. Now she continued to weave her way through the crowd on her way to the bar. She was dying of thirst; actually, as she thought about it, she was hungry. She hadn't eaten since early this morning. Dinner wouldn't be served for a while, but she figured there'd be some peanuts or something at the bar.

She spotted Steven Tydings in the corner chatting with a tall blonde. When the woman turned, laughing a little too enthusiastically at something Steven had just said, she noticed that it was Valerie Camper, another associate at the firm. Macy felt a spurt of distress. It would be just like Valerie to sleep her way to a partnership, and it didn't matter to her if she did it with a black partner or a white one. Macy though, stubbornly relied on her hard work, believing it would eventually pay off, that the partners would come to realize how good she was. It wasn't that a little butt kissing couldn't go a long way, she would gladly admit, but Macy's pride and integrity kept her from going over to Steven and joining the conversation. Her work would have to speak for itself or a promotion would mean nothing to her. Shifting direction, she tried to get to the bar by taking an alternative route.

Despite her earlier excitement, mingling was becoming a tiresome task. She had been at her desk at five-thirty that morning reviewing corporate documents for Tinsley Madison, whose father had died and left her his multi-million dollar company about which Tinsley knew nothing. Therefore, the shareholders had been robbing her blind over the last two years.

Macy had opted to skip lunch so that she could leave at three to go to the salon and get a make over. That was quickly forfeited when Steven dropped a new file on her desk, mumbling something about the guy being a very close friend of his wife and how he wanted her to take extra special care of him. When she opened the file, her first thought was, "Oh great, another deal gone sour."

Peter Thompson owned a cable company in New Jersey and had orchestrated a merger with New York's largest cable network before it was discovered that a stock-selling clause essential to his remaining in control of the company had been mistakenly left out of the contract. His previous attorney hadn't caught it and now Thompson's company was about to fold as a result of costly litigation.

She had worked until six, barely getting home in time to take a bath, style her hair and arrive at the ball at a time she considered to be fashionably late. Now she stood at the bar twirling the colorful umbrella that Skip, the bartender, had smilingly placed in her glass of orange juice.

"I'd like to dance with you."

Macy turned at the unfamiliar voice. Tall, dark and handsome didn't do justice to the male specimen that stood before her. Standing at least six feet tall, his broad shoulders were enhanced by the professional cut of the navy blue suit he wore. She guessed it was probably Versace; she knew her fashion. His hair was neatly barbered and his goatee trimmed to perfection. His skin was smooth and reminded her of melted milk chocolate. When he smiled Macy felt a slight tug in her stomach.

"Is that a question or a statement?" Macy arched one elegantly-shaped eyebrow.

"Both." Those dark eyes roamed over her, caressing her very soul right there in that crowded room.

"You expect me to agree?" Never having been able to resist a challenge, Macy decided to play with him a bit longer. She'd seen his reaction to her dress and thought she was in complete control. But he dominated the room and his intimidating form loomed over her, waiting for her response.

"I believe you will."

Arrogant and sexy, Macy knew she'd have to tread lightly.

Jordan Blake had been rated America's hottest new billionaire internationally. His cosmetics line had surpassed financial expectations and had opened the door for his growing department store chain. Just recently he had ventured into the restaurant business, and that looked just as promising as his other endeavors.

Presently, he was enjoying the exchange with this woman. Not only was she beautiful, she was also intelligent. He could tell by the way she sized him up with her eyes. He sensed that she would be no easy catch, but then again, he'd never taken the easy path before, so why start now.

As if he had witnessed their conversation, the DJ went into a slow song. The melody traveled gracefully through the room enticing several couples to take the floor in an intimate embrace. Jordan held out his hand and Macy took it. Why, she didn't know, but she did.

She should have been intimidated, if not by his bold and direct assessment of her body, but by his size. He was at least five or six inches taller than she and his broad frame clearly overwhelmed her smaller one. Still, that first touch was electric.

Jordan hadn't expected anything less. Macy, on the other hand, struggled to hide the panic that suddenly spread through her. It was just a dance, she told herself, and he was just a guy. A damn fine guy, but still, just a guy.

He held her close, one large hand resting gently at the small of her back, the other hand out to the side, giving her no room to run. His body was hard with muscle and he smelled positively dangerous. She thought about polite conversation but couldn't come up with anything intelligible.

Jordan simply wanted to close his eyes to the pleasure that coursed through him. He'd seen her first from his seat at the end of the bar. He'd watched her approach, order a drink and take a small amount of peanuts from the bowl. A gold bangle hung from her wrist.

He'd watched her intently as she laughed at something the bartender said. Enchanted by her smile, he knew he had to meet her. But what if she belonged to someone else? He had erased that notion with a shake of his head and summoned the strength to approach her.

And now he was holding her. The smooth curves of her breast rubbed gently against his ribs. The temperature in the room intensified with each gentle sway of her hips. She was so soft, so sexy.

Now that she was in his arms he could admire her more closely. Her hair was dark, streaked with a light coppery color intricately woven into a bun that sat regally atop her head and was surrounded by an array of curls, some of which had fallen from the gold clasp she wore and now brushed lightly against her neck.

Being in the cosmetics business he noted that she wore little makeup, just a hint of blush and a soft red about the lips. Her eyes were a mysterious brown, tinted with gold specks that glistened when she smiled. She was absolutely exquisite.

The dance ended and Macy stepped out of his arms before she could make a complete fool of herself. The control she'd foolishly thought she had slipped away the moment he'd touched her. Being in his arms had stirred something within her. Something she thought she'd long buried. Something that she was better off staying away from.

She returned to the bar praying that he wouldn't follow her. Though she was relieved when she turned to find that he had gone in the opposite direction, she couldn't get him out of her mind. The memory of his eyes haunted her, dark brown and mysterious, exuding an air of faint amusement. Sex appeal absolutely oozed from him.

While music and conversation bubbled around her she heard nothing. Of the hundreds of people that occupied the room, she saw no one but him. He was everywhere. He surrounded her, his smell, his voice. He clearly overwhelmed her. Putting the glass to her lips she quickly guzzled the yellow liquid and closed her eyes to find relief that was slow in coming.

"Macy? Macy? Are you listening to me?" Valerie had joined her at the bar and was chattering about something or other.

"Huh, what? Oh, hi Valerie. You're looking well this evening," she said for lack of anything else polite to say. Valerie left nothing to the imagination. Her dress was a floor-length glittering creation of green sequins with a split coming up her left leg to her upper thigh. Her breasts exploded over the top and jiggled with her every move. Yes, indeed, it was all out there on display.

"Why, thank you. But I was asking you if you'd gotten the chance to meet our newest would-be client yet," Valerie said, smiling.

"No, who might that be?" Macy gave Valerie her full attention now.

"Jordan Blake, the pretty boy millionaire. You haven't heard? What with Jade Cosmetics, his new clothing line and his chain of Italian restaurants on the West Coast, getting him as a client would be quite a coup. Steven and Richard are dying to have him sign with us. The commission would be astronomical. I just hope I get him." Valerie was practically drooling as she looked at the man who had a few moments ago held Macy spellbound.

"Is that him?" Macy asked, silently wishing it weren't.

"Yeah, isn't he gorgeous? I hear he's single too. Wouldn't that be something? Just look at him, all buff and sculpted."

Macy simply shrugged and watched Valerie who was almost salivating onto her perfectly peaked bosom.

"Imagine the things he could do with those big strong hands of his."

This remark drew Macy's attention to his hands. They did look awfully big. She blushed as she remembered their feel on her bare skin. As she shook herself free of the silliness, she admitted to herself that he was definitely fine, but so was a third of the male population. And so far that hadn't made a big difference to her.

While she was game for a good roll in the sheets every now and then, that was the extent of her involvement with men. She didn't have the time or the inclination to bother with anything beyond a few dinners, a movie and some hot steamy sex. Then maybe she'd see them for lunch here and there or they'd call just to say hi, but that's where the buck stopped, and that suited her just fine. She had goals and those goals didn't include some man bringing drama into her life. So in her book she would defer judgment on Mr. Wonderful until all the votes were in. But, damn he was one fine black man!

CHAPTER TWO

Jordan had been cornered by two of the most boring men he had ever met in his life. Steven Tydings and Richard McWinter were in the midst of giving their best sales pitch, hoping that the glitz of the ball would work to convince him that they were successful enough to handle his affairs. Steven, who was in his mid-forties, tried to sell Jordan on the finer points of the firm. Richard, who was dangerously close to sixty, felt that the room full of hired women was enough to convince him they were the best firm for the job. Jordan, however, was tired from the long trip and wanted to get back to his hotel room, as soon as possible. He hadn't even planned to attend the ball, but Steven had insisted that they continue their discussions here.

As Steven went on and on about previous clients and what they had been able to work out with them, Jordan's eyes roamed the room, searching for the woman who had intrigued him. She'd walked away so quickly; he hadn't even had the chance to ask her name.

His eyes found her at the bar again, a glass of orange juice in hand. He smiled to himself as he watched her taking small sips while trying not to scan the room for him. He knew when a woman liked him and she definitely liked him, which was a good thing because he had been quite taken with her as well.

"Steven, who's that?" Quick and to the point, was Jordan's motto.

"Who?" Steven began searching the room.

"Her, there, the one in the red." Jordan pointed to Macy.

"Oh, that's Macy Glenn. She works for the firm. She's a damn fine attorney." Steven informed Jordan. He noticed the way Jordan was looking at Macy and he fought to control the anger that coursed through him.

"An attorney?" Jordan asked. So, she was a professional woman. He'd picked up on the intelligence and the sophistication. But she also had a career. His mind was working quickly.

"Yeah, she's an associate. She handles some of our more needy clients," Richard volunteered.

"Is she married?" Jordan asked, watching as Macy continued to converse with the bartender. Whatever it was they were talking about, he had her complete attention. Jordan felt a stab of jealousy.

"No, she's not. Such a pity. I don't even think she has a boyfriend. She's always at work. Why all the questions about her? If you need a lady for the night I'm sure Steven can work something out for you." Richard nudged Steven with his elbow.

"No. I want her."

"You want her? For tonight?" Steven was both confused and agitated.

"No not for tonight." Jordan continued to watch Macy from where he stood. He didn't know for how long he wanted her, but one night definitely wouldn't be enough. Besides, he was thinking of something a little subtler to start with. Something professional. Then he'd work on the rest.

"Listen, Jordan, I don't think you understand. . ." Steven began to say. He couldn't possibly have Macy. No matter what they offered her, Macy would staunchly refuse to sleep with a client for them. And Steven certainly had his own reservations about asking her to.

"No, you listen. I want to work with her, only her. If I sign with your firm, it will be with her as my attorney. If not, I won't be signing with this firm." Jordan couldn't believe his luck. He knew he wanted this woman and he would have found a way to have her, but this was just too easy. She'd almost fallen right into his lap.

Steven's face was pale. He didn't like the way Jordan had said he *wanted* Macy. But Richard quickly intervened to close the deal.

"Whatever you want, Jordan. It's done. Macy is a good litigator. I'm sure she can handle your case. Copyright infringement is one of her strongest areas."

"I would like to speak to her now," Jordan said.

"That's fine. Shall we, Steven?" Richard said hastily. Jordan followed the two men across the room. His palms had begun to sweat and he nervously wiped them on his pants. They were so close he could hear her. She spoke slowly, melodically; her voice stroked him in all the right places.

Macy, engrossed in conversation, had not noticed their approach. When Steven touched her arm and she turned, her amber eyes instantly locked with Jordan's dark ones. The air around them fairly crackled. She could see the barely restrained fervor in his body language: his jaw clenched and he held himself stiffly as if one touch from her would make him crumble. Jordan saw the unbridled passion hidden deep within the depths of her shimmering eyes and wondered what it would be like to have her naked beneath him.

"Macy Glenn, this is Jordan Blake. He's Tydings, Banks and McWinter's newest client," Richard said, smiling. She extended her hand as she routinely did with clients, but she knew the moment he took her hand in his strong grip there would be nothing routine about their relationship. Alarm and barely contained excitement coursed through her simultaneously and she struggled to keep from pulling away.

11

"It's very nice to meet you, Ms. Glenn." His voice was like a smooth but potent wine sliding down her throat and warming her insides.

"Likewise, Mr. Blake. Welcome. I'm sure we'll do our best to please you," Macy smiled nervously.

A handshake should not have been so arousing. His blood should not have been stirring within him. He quickly withdrew his hand before he embarrassed himself by sweating on the woman or something much worse.

"Macy, Mr. Blake has requested that you be assigned to his file. Richard and I have assured him that you are competent to handle it," Steven said.

Working one on one with him? Macy gulped at the waves of panic that rippled through her. She wasn't as confident as Steven that she could do that without making a complete fool of herself. But, if the two senior partners trusted her to do this, then she would, and she'd do a damn good job too.

"Well, Mr. Blake, I thank you for your confidence in me. I can assure you that things will work out just fine. I look forward to working with you." She said all of that in one breath, silently wishing that her knees would stop wobbling.

"And I look forward to working very closely with you, Ms. Glenn," He said, caressing her with his eyes.

"Macy. Please, call me Macy," she said, taking a sip of her orange juice. Her throat had suddenly become dry.

"Okay, Macy. And you will call me Jordan." Jordan watched her tongue quickly do away with the film of juice that lay glistening on her upper lip. He almost moaned.

"Of course. Jordan, why don't you call me tomorrow morning and we'll schedule our first meeting."

"I'll call you in the morning and we'll go to lunch. You pick the place," he answered. Macy was used to demanding clients, but this statement from Jordan was different. It was a command and a dare all rolled into one, yet she couldn't very well turn him down. It was business now and business came first. Even though warning bells were ringing in her head, she turned a deaf ear to them and, like the pro she was, smiled and agreed.

CHAPTER THREE

Why she took so much time mulling over what she was going to wear to work the next day was a puzzle to her. The tan suit was too boring and the blue was too conservative. She finally opted for the long ivory skirt with the fuchsia blouse and matching ivory jacket. This was both cool and sensible. Who cared if Jordan liked it or not? Who was she kidding? She had thought about him all night long. Lord, but he was beautiful.

She arrived at the office shortly after eight, which was a bit late and highly unlike her. Katy, her secretary, handed her messages as soon as she came in. There were seven in total. As she flipped through them she noticed that they were all from Jordan.

"He seems pretty anxious to talk to you," Katy said, reading the expression on her boss's face.

"I would say so. Get him on the phone for me," she slipped out of her jacket and into the soft leather executive chair and began looking through his file that had been placed on her desk.

"Don't make that call just yet, Katy. I need to speak with Macy first." Steven walked into Macy's office and closed the door.

"What's the matter? Did he change his mind?" Somewhat unnerved, she rose to look Steven in the eye.

"No, it's nothing like that. Sit down, Macy." As he waited for her to sit back down, Macy could see the look of distress on his face. Steven was tall, slim and quietly handsome in his dark suit and shining wing-tipped shoes. She remembered a time when his looks had just about melted her heart. Now there was only business.

"What is it, Steven?"

"Macy, how dedicated are you to your job?"

What was going on? "Steven, I don't think you need to ask that question. I mean, really, just because I came in a little later than usual is no reason to question my loyalty or dedication," Macy began.

"No, no it's nothing like that. It's just that Blake is a big client, and the partners and I wish to impress that upon you before you meet with him." Steven relaxed in the chair across from her desk.

"Oh, is that all? Steven, I know the drill. Whatever he wants as long as he signs the retainer." Macy felt her own muscles beginning to relax.

"Well, Macy, that's not all this time. This is a delicate situation. Did you know that Blake's father is rumored to have connections with the Mafia?" Steven said matter-of-factly.

"What? He's not Italian, he's as black as I am," She felt confused. However she had noted the fine wavy hair that had fairly glistened atop his head.

"He's only half Italian. His mother was black. After he graduated from college he changed his name from Jordan Penelli to Jordan Blake, his mother's maiden name. His father is now head of the Penelli family, which is a very big deal in these parts."

"So what? Are we indebted to the mob for something? I don't understand what this has to do with anything. And I can assure you that I'll do my best to get Mr. Blake through this lawsuit in one piece and as unscathed as possible," Macy said.

"Good. I mean, we just want to make him happy at any cost. That's where you come in." Steven slipped off the thin gold-framed glasses he wore and rubbed his eyes.

"I know my job, Steven, and I plan to do it." She felt comfortable talking to Steven even though he was a senior partner. First and foremost he was a friend; he had always been a friend to her, even after all they'd been through. Sometimes she thought if only he hadn't gotten married. . . . But that was neither here nor there. She watched him sit back in the chair and smooth out his designer tie. Then he toyed with the moustache that he'd just recently let grow in. He was normally clean-shaven but this was a good look for him. He had a darker complexion than Macy and his eyes were like dots of coal as he replaced his glasses.

"Well, it seems that he is hell bent on you representing him exclusively which means that your other files will be reassigned," Steven announced.

"That's ridiculous. I am perfectly capable of handling him along with my usual workload."

"He insists that he be your only client. In fact, he called Richard and Max this morning." Macy felt coldness come over her. Maxwell Banks was the senior partner, and if a client had contact with him, then he was definitely a big client.

"Max called me and asked that I be the one to tell you since I work closer with you than the others." Steven waited watching the severity of the situation sink in.

"Since we're both black and they're not," Macy added.

"Yeah, something like that," Steven chuckled. Macy always kept it real. "He wants you in L.A. tomorrow morning. Your flight arrangements have been made. You can work out of the L.A. office; my secretary's arranging for an apartment for you close to Blake's Beverly Hills mansion." Steven knew she would take it hard but he wasn't prepared for her calm, quiet voice.

She carefully masked the extent of her anger. "Are you out of your mind? This is my home! This is my office! Do you propose that I uproot myself and leave my family to be near this man? What is he, some kind of control freak or something?" She was nearing a more reckless reaction but she tried to rein herself in.

"Macy, you need to understand, this is a big deal for us and a big deal for us could ultimately lead to a big deal for you. Don't tell me you don't want a partnership because I can see it in everything you do. And this would really impress the senior partners."

"Don't you dare try to bribe me, Steven. You know perfectly well that all my hard work is so that one day I can make partner. But this is insane. I can represent Blake just as well from New York as I can in L.A. Doesn't he understand that?"

"He doesn't want to understand that. He has made his decision. Now we have to accommodate him to get the business."

"How long do I have to stay?" Macy asked, amazed that she was even considering such a plan.

"Indefinitely. Permanently," Steven shrugged his shoulders.

"This is the most ridiculous thing I have ever heard. . ." The explosion hit. She couldn't take it any longer. She leaped out of her chair and paced the floor. Anger roiled through her, hot and thick.

"Macy, it's not that bad. I mean, what do you have here? Your mother and sister are over forty miles away. And you're at the office more than you are at your apartment. So what's the big deal?"

"*What's the big deal? What's the big deal?*" She was losing it and fast. She picked up a stack of magazines from the coffee table and hurled them across the room.

"The big deal is, I'm the one getting screwed here. Is this some little test of my loyalty? I've worked my butt off for the last five years, and all I get in return is being shipped to the West Coast because Mr. Mafia wants me there! Why do you care so much about him and so little about me?" Katy opened the door to see if things were okay. When she saw more magazines flying through the air, she wisely closed the door and returned to her desk.

"I told you before, he makes a lot of money, and a good portion of that money will be ours if we represent him competently. Now, Max has every confidence that you can do this and do it well enough to keep our client happy and make a truckload of money for us in the process."

"In the end I guess everything comes down to money. Silly of me to think that maybe, just maybe, I'd have a little say in decisions being made about my life. But I see it's all about the firm as usual."

"You made it all about the firm when you decided to set your sites on being partner. It's not that bad Macy. Besides, you know damn well that if Max didn't think you could do this he wouldn't send you, regardless of Blake's request."

"Blake can go to hell, and for asking me to do this, you can follow him." Macy screamed.

"Macy, the bottom line is, if you want your job, if you care anything about the work you've done for the past five years, you'll go to L.A. The firm will move you and your belongings and pay you a substantial bonus, but if you turn down this opportunity, you might as well kiss that partnership goodbye. You'll become our resident ambulance chaser. And your career, hell, Max can destroy that with one phone call. You really have no choice." Steven said preparing to leave.

"You are a pathetic excuse for a man. You and all the other men who have just an inch of power. I hate you all." Macy finally stopped pacing and plopped down on the couch, burying her face in her hands.

"Come on, Macy, its not that bad. One day you'll thank me for pushing you into this." He smiled.

"Get out!" She shouted as she searched the room for something else to throw. Steven was out the door before she had any success.

Jordan had decided that lunch in his hotel suite would be best. After his decision to take Macy back to L.A. with him, he had decided that, not knowing what her reaction might be; something a little more private might be appropriate. She would surely want to know the details of this new arrangement. He had called her secretary and left the suite number and time she should arrive. Now he was dressing in a black Armani with a heavily starched white shirt and purple silk tie. He wanted to appear as professional as possible.

The table was set and he was anxiously awaiting her arrival. He had lain awake all night thinking about her, about her lips, her neck, her ears, her legs. He could concentrate on nothing but her. When the front desk called to let him know that she was being escorted to his suite, his hands began to sweat.

Macy stepped from the elevator seething with anger. When Katy had given her the message, it was all she could do to keep from calling him and telling him where he could go, and the shortest route to get there. But as Steven had said, she really had no choice. This was her career. She would go to L.A. and represent him so well that an offer of partnership from the firm would be pretty much guaranteed. If she could only get through this lunch without strangling him first. It was hard enough for a black woman in corporate America without a black man trying to pull her strings. Any attraction she felt for this man had been killed the minute Steven told her of his stupid request. Now, he was just a client. This whole situation was business and Macy would make the best of it.

He opened the door and her heart stopped. So much for the "just business" facade. He loomed over her small frame. Her earlier estimate was incorrect; he was definitely taller than six feet, or at least it seemed that way compared to her own five feet three inches. Though he looked ominous and mean, there was depth within his eyes and a kind of sadness.

"Hello, Macy. It's nice to see you again," he said smoothly, giving her his best smile.

"Hello, Mr. Blake. I got your message," Macy replied coolly. She ignored the way that smile tugged at her heart.

"Please come in. I thought we decided that you'd call me Jordan," He escorted her to her seat at the elegantly decorated table.

"No, you *told* me that I would call you Jordan. But nonetheless, Jordan it is," She kept her eyes as level with his as she could without giving herself a neck cramp.

"Have a seat." He motioned toward the chair across from his. "You're looking exceptionally well today. Pink is a good color for you," he said, noting that the compliment had caught Macy off guard.

"Thank you," she stammered and took her seat.

"Our lunch should be up in a minute. Is there anything you would like to know about your new position?" he asked as he poured her a glass of wine. Macy detested red wine, and she most certainly didn't drink in the middle of the day.

"My new position? If you're asking if I have any objections to your ridiculous request, the answer is no. If you're wondering if I came here to ask you to reconsider, you're sorely mistaken." She pushed her glass to the side.

"I don't think they explained everything to you."

"What else is there to explain?" she asked calmly.

"Well, you'll be my personal attorney, of sorts. Of course you will do something about this copyright infringement that Paris, my previous attorney, has gotten me into, and aside from that, you will handle all of my legal issues, contracts, lawsuits, trademarks, everything. You will handle these things exclusively. My administrative assistant will report to you, and my daily schedule, meetings and things of that nature will be left up to your approval." He thought he saw a flash of anger in her eyes, but quickly dismissed it.

"I believe what you really need is a secretary, not an attorney."

"Drink your wine," he said, ignoring her assessment of the job description. "I am aware of what I need, but I'm also aware of what I want." Once again he motioned toward the glass that she had pushed aside.

"I don't drink during the day. And what exactly is it that you want?" Propping her chin up on the elbow that rested on the table, Macy eyed him suspiciously.

"I want you," It was a simple statement and yet it held so much power. He sat back in his chair and stared at her, almost undressing her with his eyes while she processed his response.

"What do you mean, you want me? You mean to work for you right?" Instinctively, she knew that she was wrong, that business was not the extent of this relationship for him.

"It's an excellent year, you must taste it. I want you to handle my business affairs, yes, but I'd like the opportunity to get to know you better." He lowered the glass back to the table and waited for her next question. He noted a subtle mix of fury and astounding sexuality in her, and his blood began to boil.

"I said I don't drink during the day. And stop confusing me with all this talk about wine. I'm here for business reasons and that's all. As a matter of fact, I really don't see why I'm being forced to move across the country to provide legal services that could just as easily be provided in New York."

"It's simple, Macy. I want you with me. So you need to move to the other side of the country, as I do not live in New York. I stated as much to Max and he thought it was an excellent idea." Rising from his seat he circled the table, stopping to stand behind her. The soft curls from last night fell at her shoulders now and he toyed with one momentarily as she began to speak.

"Look, Mr. Blake, I am an attorney and for the last five years I have been very successful in representing my clients' best interests. But I am not now nor will I ever be someone's personal assistant. I understand that you are very, let's say, influential with the partners at my firm, so I will do my best to work with you. But make no mistake about it! I will not be scheduling any appointments for you, nor will I be coordinating any of your other personal tasks! Do I make myself perfectly clear?" A steady stream of heat had begun to rise within her as he lightly brushed against her skin. Long, sleek fingers had gently lifted her hair during her little tirade and were now massaging the tense neck muscles underneath. "And stop touching me, damnit! It's inappropriate!" Swatting his hands away she watched the look of bemusement on his face.

"We can work out the details once we're in L.A. Now drink some wine. Our lunch will be here in just a second," He walked over to the phone, but the doorbell rang, stopping him from making the phone call to room service. Macy took note of his confident stride. He was one arrogant SOB, she thought to herself. His taut muscles strained against the material of his suit jacket, causing her to wonder how they would feel beneath her fingers. What was she thinking? He was the most infuriating man. She didn't know how she would possibly be able to work with him. And what was with the wine? Was it spiked or something?

A cloth-covered cart with silver topped plates and more wine was wheeled into the room. No one spoke as the bellhop removed each top to display its delectable contents before turning to leave the room.

The food smelled wonderful. There was chicken breast stuffed with sautéed vegetables set atop a mountain of wild rice. Macy was starving. They ate in silence for the first ten minutes. Then, as Macy had expected, he asked her about the wine again.

"Did you put something in my wine?" She eyed him suspiciously.

"No, I just don't like to drink alone." He smiled again, giving her a view of his gleaming white teeth.

"Well, I already told you I don't drink during the day. And I don't drink red wine, so you might want to keep that in mind the next time you decide to offer me a drink." Macy wanted to finish this lunch and leave. She put another forkful of food into her mouth.

Jordan watched her chew and lick her lips. He remembered this from last night; it was the most sensual movement he had ever seen. What would it feel like to have that tongue gracefully gliding over his skin?

"Macy, you are a very beautiful woman." That simple statement warmed her to the tips of her toes. This man thought she was beautiful. The wine had to be spiked. He was her client, however, and hard as it was, she had to maintain a professional relationship with him.

"Jordan, I don't think comments like that are appropriate. I would appreciate it if we could maintain a business-like relationship," She sounded unconvincing even to herself, and he certainly didn't miss the underlying tone of her statement.

"And how long do you think we can do that, Macy? I don't usually beat around the bush, so I won't start now. I am very attracted to you, and I'm fairly sure that you're having the same reaction towards me. But if you need some time to adjust to the newness of the situation, then I'll oblige you, *this time*." He gave her a smile as brilliant as the rest of him.

"Before we go any further I think we should get something straight. I am your attorney. You are the client. That's it."

Jordan sat back in the chair watching her closely.

"And the next time you feel the need to be honest about your attraction to me or get the urge to touch me, think again, cause I'll be on the next plane back to New York regardless of my job. Do I make myself clear?"

A casual nod of the head was all he gave in response.

"What time is our flight?" Macy said, desperate to change the subject.

"It's at ten this evening. Will you be packed?"

"Yeah, sure. The firm is going to take care of moving my apartment. I just need to pack my clothes and make some phone calls. So I'll be going now. I guess I'll meet you at the airport," Macy got out of her chair and started moving towards the door.

"No. I'll pick you up at nine." Because Jordan hadn't turned in his chair, Macy got a good look at his thick ebony hair, the way it tapered off sleekly down his neck. Yeah, she thought he had mixed heritage. His hair was too good and it shone like a raven's wing. What would it feel like between her fingers? she wondered.

"L.A. must have a wealth of beautiful men." She could have kicked herself for letting that slip out.

"Actually I was born in Sicily. My mother was African-American and my father is Sicilian." When she saw Jordan start to shift in his chair, she turned to walk toward the door so he wouldn't see her flustered state.

He was out of the chair and behind her before she could reach for the doorknob.

"Well, I guess I'll see you later." Slowly, he turned her to face him. They were so close Macy found it hard to breath. His hands rested on either side of her neck as his eyes burned into hers.

"You're touching me again," she reminded him.

Snatching his hands away, he smiled at her. "I look forward to working with you, Macy. I'm sure this is going to be a pleasurable experience."

"Yes, it will be." That was all she could say. His touch was making too many thoughts run through her mind at one time. Nearly running to the elevator, she fought the urge to go back into that room and finish what he'd started. A mixture of pride and fear kept her feet planted firmly as she pushed the down button. The doors opened into the lobby, she promptly stepped off and darted out the door.

CHAPTER FOUR

On a dark winding road on the outskirts of Las Vegas a black Chevy Camaro was found on the rocks at the bottom of a forty-foot high cliff. A male body was crouched in the driver's seat where he had bled to death from a wound to his head. Only an hour before, a man had stood on the edge of the cliff watching as the vehicle hit the rocky bottom. Satisfied, he'd gone back to his sports utility vehicle, lit a cigarette and ridden away.

Though Macy had arrived back at her Manhattan apartment an hour earlier, she had yet to put a single stitch of clothing into her suitcase. Her mind reeled with the realization that she was going to pack up and move across the country with this man. This man that she had met a mere fifteen hours ago. What was going on? All she had ever wanted was to be an attorney, to work at a reputable firm and to make a name for herself. None of this entailed gallivanting across the country with some spoiled, rich egomaniac. She paced the floor, wondering if she should call Steven. As she picked up the receiver, she thought of what she'd say. She'd tell him what to do with his ultimatum and then she'd call Blake and tell him the same thing. And then she'd be fired. She'd have to start all over again at some less than spectacular firm, which would pay her peanuts because she'd been released from Tydings. Her name would be disgraced and her father would be disappointed. She dropped the phone back into its cradle, grabbed an armful of clothes from her top drawer and began to stuff them into her suitcase.

On the plane they sat next to each other. Jordan had politely given Macy the window seat. Though she tried to pass the time by staring out into the clouds, her mind kept wandering back to the man beside her. She definitely did not want to converse with him. He smelled too good. She wasn't sure if it was his cologne or just his manly scent. Whatever it was, it was wreaking havoc on her hormones.

Jordan had booked their flight in first class, of course. The seats were leather and seemed to be designed for comfort. Hoping to relax, Macy leaned back in her seat, closed her eyes and propped her arms on the armrests. Apparently, Jordan had the same idea. When their arms met there was instant friction, and the interior of the plane suddenly seemed a hundred degrees warmer. She quickly moved her arm, hoping that he hadn't noticed her reaction.

Jordan had not only noticed it but was feeling a little heated himself. He still couldn't believe that she was upset about his generous offer. What was wrong with this woman? Earlier at lunch he'd thought she was literally going to attack him.

"Macy, can we please try and clear the air? Our relationship will go much more smoothly if we can at least be civil to each other."

"Our business relationship, Mr. Blake, will work out just fine." They were back to Mr. Blake again. She was still pissed with him.

"Why are you so determined to dislike me? Have I done something to offend you?" he asked.

"You can't be serious! As I may have neglected to mention earlier back in your hotel room, I do not appreciate your deciding that I would agree to this ludicrous arrangement you've made. And yes, you have offended me. You thought so very little of me that you failed to discuss this with me first. Or is that the way you usually operate?"

A conversation with her mother had revived Macy's anger. She had called her mother to explain what was going on, and her mother, strangely enough, thought the move was a good idea.

"It's time for a change, Macy. You're not gettin' any younger and maybe you can even find a husband while you're out there and make me some grandbabies,"

Macy should have expected that last remark. Her mother had been dropping little hints about having grandchildren for a while now. Her sister Leigh was still in college, so it was out of the question for her to have kids anytime in the near future.

But if she were honest with herself, she'd have to admit that that was not the total cause of her anger now. She was angry with herself for actually being attracted to Jordan, and even angrier for allowing him to tell her that she was attracted. He didn't know her that well. She tried to rationalize the attraction by reminding herself that it was probably caused by her lack of male companionship. She couldn't remember the last time she had been intimate with someone.

"I'm sorry if my hiring methods were a bit out of the ordinary, but when I want something, I go get it." He shrugged, "It's a habit."

"Even, if that something is a person, a living, breathing, human being? Never mind, don't answer that. Let's just drop the subject. I don't have much choice so I'd like to forget about it," Macy turned back to the window. Of course she did have a choice, she thought.

She could choose to be unemployed. She could choose to throw her career away. She could choose those things and walk away from this man. Or she could try to rise to the challenge. Obviously she was choosing the latter.

They continued the rest of the flight in silence. When they stopped over in Kansas to refuel Jordan disappeared, leaving Macy to sit in the crowded airport lobby alone. When he returned, he had two cinnamon rolls and a bouquet of yellow roses. Macy's anger melted away. He was trying, so she ought to do the same.

"Thank you, Jordan," She bent her head to the roses and breathed in their fragrance.

"I apologize for any grief I may have caused you. I hope that we can put the last few hours behind us and be friends," Jordan lied. He wanted much more than a friendship, but he realized that that admission at this point would sabotage his chances.

"I think that would be nice." Every smart retort Macy had in her mind vanished. The cinnamon rolls were just like she liked them, hot and gooey with icing. Even though she had been eating with her fork, she'd still managed to get a substantial amount of that icing on her fingers. Before she could reach for a napkin Jordan grabbed her wrist and lowered his head. Gently he sucked the sweet confection from each finger, all the while watching her eyes grow languid in response.

"Thank you, but the next time I'll use a napkin." Swallowing the passion that had threatened to surface, Macy snatched her hand away and headed for the boarding gate. Jordan smiled as he watched her hasty retreat.

They arrived in L.A. in the early morning hours of a Saturday. Macy was asleep when the plane landed and Jordan had gently awakened her. She was still half asleep as he led her to the car and helped her into the backseat. He surprised her by getting in the back with her, putting his arms around her and pulling her head to his shoulder. She promptly fell back asleep.

When she awoke again, the car was making its way through tall iron gates and proceeding up a steep hill. A massive gray stone house sat between massive trees. Jordan's home was as beautiful as he was. Pansies, snapdragons, and clematis filled flowerbeds. Around the house itself, climbing and shrub roses in brilliant colors stood guard.

When the car pulled up in front of the door, a slender black woman looking to be in her early forties came out to greet them.

Jordan got out and said something to the woman, then reached into the car to help Macy out. She took a deep breath of the rose-scented air and cast an admiring glance around her. Then the woman she took to be the housekeeper smiled at her and took her hand, leading her into the foyer.

Gleaming black marble floors led to a large winding staircase of black lacquer. African American art adorned the walls. Among the paintings was one of her personal favorites.

"You know this piece?" Jordan asked seeing her enchantment with the picture.

"James Porter, *Gate of Zaire*. It's beautiful. No matter how many times I see it, it still moves me."

"Yeah, I have several of Porter's pieces."

"What is this?" Her fingers gently grazed a colorful plate on a marble pedestal.

"Oh, that's a *Blue Monday* plate. I frequent the Wilson Art Gallery, and saw these once in the gift shop. I thought they were exceptionally done so I purchased a few sets." He pointed to another dozen or so sets mounted on similar pedestals.

Macy's eyes roamed throughout the room. Surveying the rest of his plate collection she admitted, "They have a lot of character. They're nice. I like it," she said finally.

"Why thank you for your approval, Ms. Glenn." For some reason he was genuinely pleased that she approved of his home.

"You're most welcome, Mr. Blake." Macy felt herself staring into those mystifying eyes again, wondering what was beneath the hard exterior of this man. Then she noticed her bags being brought in. "Why are my bags being brought in? I'm scheduled for a hotel," she questioned.

"I thought you could stay here until your apartment is ready."

Macy stared at him skeptically.

"There are twenty rooms in this house, Macy. I'm sure we won't bump into each other too much, if that's what you're worried about." He pulled her aside so that the driver could pass with her bags.

"Just take them to the Peach Room, Joseph," Jordan said to the tall man who had picked them up at the airport.

Macy couldn't wait to see the 'Peach Room.' It sounded both silly and interesting. She had started to follow Joseph up the steps when Jordan's voice stopped her.

"Macy?" She turned to see him standing with his legs slightly apart and his hands in his pockets. He looked like a nervous teenager on a first date. "Yes, Jordan?"

"Do you want something to eat? I know you haven't had anything in a while," Jordan was feeling unusually nervous himself. Now that he had gotten her to L.A., he would be working hard to win her over, and he didn't want to mess things up in any way. Tread lightly, he thought.

"Yeah, I guess that would be nice. But I think I'll take a shower and a quick nap first. Is that okay?" Macy said in a small voice. She was suddenly very shy.

"That's fine. I'll have Emma wake you at. . ."

The woman, whom she supposed was Emma, came running into the room, her face pale with horror. "Mr. Jordan, sir, the phone . . . it's about your brother. It's about Matthew!" She was screaming.

Jordan walked briskly into the other room. Macy's curiosity demanded that she follow him. On a table near the window he picked up the cordless phone and began to speak. She saw the tensing of his jaw as he spoke in hushed tones to the person on the other end of the phone line. When he gently placed the receiver in its cradle he sat down heavily on the big sofa. He looked absolutely horrified. Macy was at his side in an instant.

CHAPTER FIVE

"Jordan, what is it?" Macy placed a reassuring arm around his shoulder.

"It's Matthew. He's gone. He drove his car off a cliff in Vegas. It exploded on impact." His eyes were dark pools now, impossible to read. Macy instinctively hugged him.

"Oh, Jordan, I'm so sorry. Were you and he close."

"He was my only family." Jordan hugged her to him so tightly it was difficult for her to breathe. She understood his need all too well. Memories of her father's death still haunted her. They sat silently locked in each other's arms for a while longer. Finally, Jordan released her and lay back against the sofa, closing his eyes.

Placing a comforting hand on his arm Macy waited until he was ready to speak.

"He was the only family I had left. My friend, my confidant." His voice was full of the grief that consumed him. "We've been through so much together. . ."

"Shhh. I understand. I lost my father a few years ago. I know exactly what you're going through."

He reached out to her, glad that she was there with him. Macy went to him, eager to offer what comfort she could. Seeing the human side of Jordan for the first time was both soothing and disturbing.

Clearly he wasn't the arrogant, self-centered person she'd been trying to convince herself he was. But then again, this human person, the one that could be hurt, was even more attractive than she'd imagined.

"Mr. Jordan sir, there's a detective on the phone for you. He says it's about Matthew,"

"Thank you, Emma."

Jordan's conversation did not last long. The phone was placed none too gently into the cradle as he raked his hands through his hair. Thick black eyebrows were drawn together when he faced Macy. "I must go to Sicily." His voice was clipped as he struggled to maintain control of the fury that burned inside of him.

"What? Why?"

"It's complicated. Detective Marshall says that he believes Matthew was dead before the car ran off the cliff. If that's the case, then its murder, and I have to find out who did it and why,"

"I'm confused, isn't that the detective's job? Why should you personally get involved?" Macy felt alarmed.

"Because he was my brother and because my father might have had something to do with this,"

"I thought you said Matthew was your only family?" Macy was confused.

"He was the only family that I claimed. My father lives in Sicily."

"Okay, so why don't you claim your father?"

"That's a long story." He said in a voice that let her know he had no intention of telling her anymore about that situation.

"Alright, so why do you think he's involved?" She'd save the disowning of his father for later.

"You are certainly full of questions, my little Macy," Jordan tried to smile.

"I'm sorry, I don't mean to intrude. I've always been curious."

"Will you come with me?"

"Me? Why would you want me there?"

"I have to find out what happened to Matthew. If my father was involved, I need to know." His tone reflected both his fear and determination. "And besides, Sicily is a beautiful place. Have you ever been?"

"No. But I don't understand why you would want me there. It's clearly not going to be a vacation, and I'm sure you won't be needing any legal advice on the trip." Fighting the conflict that roiled inside of her, Macy tried to stay professional.

"That is true. But I feel strangely serene when you're near. Please say you'll come." His eyes pleaded with her. How could she say no?

"Let's not jump the gun. It may still turn out to be just an accident." She hoped.

"I doubt it," Jordan said.

"Why do you doubt it? What makes you so sure it was murder and that your father had something to do with it?"

"Because my mother died the same way. When I was twenty-one she was in her car and it went off a cliff in Montana. Just like Matthew. Sound familiar?"

"Did they rule that a murder?"

"No, but I've always suspected some sort of cover-up. It was just too painful to deal with so I put it out of my mind. But, I know there's a connection and I need to put all the pieces together." Remembering what Steven had said about Jordan's father being a big Mafia man, Macy feared Jordan might be next.

"Jordan, you don't think that . . . that maybe . . . um . . . well you could be. . ." She stumbled over the words.

"That I could be next? No, I hadn't thought of that. That's all the more reason to get to the bottom of this and soon."

This was too much for Macy. She had just met Jordan two days ago and all of a sudden she was living with him in his mansion and on her way to helping him solve the murder of his mother and brother. What was she doing?

"I don't think I like this very much, Jordan." As if he sensed her distress he gathered her in his arms and held her close. This was definitely more than she had bargained for. Pulling away she put some space between them.

"Maybe I should go and take that nap now," she said grasping the arm of the chair to steady herself. His kisses were toxic and she had to fight a serious battle with herself to keep him at arms length.

Feeling her retreat he wondered if he should push. In any case, now was not the time. There were other things he needed to deal with. The fire that burned for Macy would have to be banked until he could get things in order.

Macy awoke in the Peach Room, which was accurately named. Peach was everywhere, tastefully done though, as was the rest of the house. The four-poster brass bed and the six pillows that adorned it were covered in peach pillowcases to match the peach comforter and silk sheets. The carpet was white with orange throw rugs scattered about. There was a brass dressing table and a soft peach couch that sat off to one corner. A big bay window was at the other corner of the room and peach pillows were strewn on the window sill, providing a comfortable place to sit. After they had eaten breakfast yesterday, Jordan had taken her on a grand tour. She had seen the Blue Room, the Red Room, the White Room and the Peach Room and Jordan's room, which was almost totally black from the walls to the carpet. This room was dismal and stifling; it seemed nothing at all like Jordan.

In an effort to keep his mind off of Matthew until he had further news from the police, Jordan arranged for Macy to meet Paris, his longtime friend and former attorney. Macy had tried to discuss specifics of Jordan's prior contracts with the company that was now suing him, but quickly realized the reason Jordan had come looking for help. Paris clearly had no idea what he was doing. That, she figured, would work to her advantage because she would have no interference in her dealings on Jordan's behalf. They enjoyed a late lunch at a nice little bistro that Jordan liked. She had to admit the man's good taste was evident in everything he did.

He dressed impeccably, ate at the best places, and his house was gorgeous, all decorated by him personally. She wondered how he had achieved all of this alone. And how in the hell had he remained single for so long. Why some woman hadn't wrapped him around her finger by now was a mystery to Macy. She briefly thought of herself as that woman but quickly pushed the idea out of her mind. That was silly; she wasn't interested in a serious relationship.

At first, she had wondered why this man had been so appealing to her and now she knew why. Not only was he fine to look at but he seemed to be a fine person on the inside as well, despite his bossiness. That, to Macy, was his only major downfall.

Although he was quiet about making decisions for her, he made them nonetheless - deciding that she would come here to work, and then that she would stay at his house until her apartment was ready, and now planning their meetings as well as their meals. He definitely liked to be in control. The trouble was Macy did too. Or so she thought. It seemed that since she'd met him she had been relinquishing that control, bits at a time.

Today she was reading through a few new contracts that had been sent to Paris while Jordan had been away. Since she had been told once again to do this, she thought that she would enjoy making Jordan sit there with her while she did it. But that idea was quickly deflated when Emma told her at breakfast that Mr. Jordan had gotten an early start and was already out of the house. She had no idea where he had gone. Her spirits sagged a bit and the contracts lost all their appeal.

Leaving the stack of papers where they lay on the small table in her room she closed the door behind her and wandered through the big house alone, not really looking for anything in particular, just walking around. Jordan was everywhere. His scent permeated through each room. From the expensive window treatments to the throw rugs that matched the furniture perfectly, his signature was apparent throughout the house.

On the first level, beyond the rooms that Emma and Joseph occupied, she noticed another room that she hadn't visited yesterday. Jordan had taken great care to show her the house; she was somewhat surprised that they had missed this room. She opened the door slowly but couldn't see inside because it was so dark. She walked in, straining her eyes to locate a light switch. She made out what looked like a kerosene lamp. As she ran her hand across the fixture it abruptly came alive, casting a dim light across the room. In the muted illumination she looked around. The painted wooden casement ceilings looked like something out of a 14th century pamphlet that she had seen in the interior decorator's office when she was trying to decorate her own office. Even though this period seemed in stark contrast to the theme of the rest of the house, that wasn't half as strange as the weapons collection that lined the walls. There was everything from swords to rifles to an old musket that reminded Macy of the pilgrims at Plymouth Rock. Along the other wall were more updated artillery, a silver handgun and guns of pure black metal. She wasn't sure of the names of them all but she had seen them in the movies. What was this? Did Jordan have a penchant for weaponry? It appeared he did.

She didn't like it in here, and she was suddenly glad that Jordan hadn't shown her this room. Before she could turn to leave, she sensed another presence. By the increased thumping of her heart she knew that it could only be one person.

Without turning around, she greeted him warmly. "Hello, Jordan. I see you returned early."

"I wanted to spend some time with my favorite attorney." This was true for the most part. After arranging for Matthew's remains to be cremated, he'd felt dismal and alone. She was just what he needed to keep going; otherwise, his grief would very well consume him. "I see you've made yourself at home." Entranced by the way the soft light seemed to dance in her hair, Jordan moved to stand closer.

Macy thought she heard a hint of annoyance in his tone. "I was just wandering around." That sounded innocent enough, she thought.

"And you just happened to wander down here?" One smooth glossy eyebrow was drawn in question. He shifted to rest against the wall, inches away from Macy. In blue jeans and a Yankees T-shirt he was the sexiest man she had ever seen.

Butterflies danced throughout Macy's stomach, "Yup, it seems that way. Was this room supposed to be off limits or something?"

"No, not at all." A small smile tugged at his lips.

Feeling a bit more relaxed Macy asked, "So what's the deal with the minor arsenal you've assembled?"

"Nothing special, just a hobby." Dismissing the contents of the room, he continued. "Besides, I have some minor work related changes that I want to discuss with you."

"Well, I am here to work," she admitted.

He didn't speak. He just stared, stirring her insides until she thought she'd collapse at his feet. That look of interest, of primal lust, heightened her own growing desire and suddenly she felt very bold.

What would Jordan Blake do if she began coming on to him, as he had done with her. She stood on her tiptoes to remove a piece of something from his hair. Her eyes never leaving his face, she placed her open palm in the middle of his chest and let it sit there for a moment. His heart beat slow and steady beneath her skin. She lowered her hand to his stomach and could see his eyes begin to darken. It was too late to rethink this foolish game she had begun; his reaction was swift. Her scalp tingled as his fingers raked through her hair. He claimed her mouth with a fierce passion. Their tongues met and clashed; it was like an erupting volcano. The barrette that she had used to hold her hair together hit the floor with a clinking sound that went unheard. As the kiss deepened Jordan heard the soft moans coming from deep within her. His hand went through her hair and down the back of her neck. She had never tasted anything as sweet as his kiss. It was intoxicating. She would swear she had never really been kissed until now.

"*Ti adoro. Comè sei Bella.*"

She heard Jordan mumbling something but she couldn't understand it. A black man speaking a foreign language was overwhelmingly erotic. It didn't matter what he had said, just the sound of his voice and the feel of him so close was enough. They ended the kiss reluctantly and struggled to catch their breath. Holding her close, he whispered the words again. Macy could stand it no longer.

"What are you saying?"

"Nothing and everything." His voice was husky with bridled passion. If only he could explain to her what was going on inside him. Hell, he had yet to come to terms with it himself. All he knew was that he wanted her. He needed her. The rest seemed irrelevant.

"Tell me what it means. Is it Italian?" Macy leaned back so she could look into his eyes – eyes that said so much and yet said nothing.

"Yes, my sweet Macy. It's Italian." Jordan chuckled at the perplexed look on her face.

"That's not fair. I don't speak Italian."

"I just said that you are beautiful, Macy. Must you know everything?" Jordan kissed the tip of her nose.

"Yes, I must. I don't think that's all you said either, but I'll figure it out myself."

"Maybe you should try learning the language since it seems we'll be leaving as soon as it can be arranged." Jordan waited for her response. He was prepared to get on his knees and beg her to go with him if necessary.

"What about my work? I can't just leave. I have to find an apartment and get my office situated and. . ." Macy stopped speaking as he stared at her calmly. *He didn't, he wouldn't do that to her again.* "Please, don't tell me that you made a phone call to New York?"

"Okay, I won't tell you," he said smiling.

"Dammit Jordan, you cannot run my life! Why don't you understand that?" Macy was not really upset but felt she should argue the point anyway, just on principle. The thought of going to Sicily with him was very appealing. She was coming to realize that the mere thought of being with him was appealing; Sicily was just an added perk.

"I am not running your life, Macy. I merely made a phone call that I knew you would make a big deal out of making yourself. I am trying to be considerate here. You women are always wanting a man to consider your feelings and now that I'm doing that, you're complaining."

"Considerate, my ass!" Macy almost yelled.

"Such ugly language coming from such a beautiful mouth. I want to take care of you Macy. Why can't you calm down and let me do that?"

"Because I can take care of myself. I am the attorney and you are the client, Jordan. There is no need for you to take care of me."

"I understand that there is no need for it, but I wish to do it anyway. Please try and get used to it," he said as he turned away from her. "I hope you haven't unpacked yet. I told Joseph I wanted the first flight out of L.A.," and he walked out of the room.

Alone again, she thought that just a few days ago she had been a prosperous litigation attorney going about the daily tasks of her life. Now she was living in a mansion with one of the world's wealthiest, and by far most attractive men she'd ever seen, and she was contemplating going across the ocean with him while he attempted to solve a murder. Shaking her head, she tried to maintain a semblance of control.

Instead, she remembered the kiss they'd just shared, the intimacy of the moment. Somehow she knew that there was much more to come in her dealings with Jordan.

Jordan went to his room smiling to himself. He had known Macy would be sweet, known it from the first time he had laid eyes on her. But his estimate had been sorely lacking; she was beyond sweet, she was beyond imagination. He wished he could completely concentrate on her and make Macy his, but there were other, more pressing matters he needed to deal with.

Attempting to concentrate on the matter at hand he thought of the autopsy results Detective Marshall had given him earlier that day. They had confirmed that Matthew Penelli died of blunt trauma to the head, and that he was dead well before the explosion. This fact did not surprise Jordan, but it did worry him. After speaking with

Detective Marshall, he had been more convinced than ever of what he must do.

Dioncello Penelli was involved in his brother's murder, and Jordan would prove it. *But what about Macy,* he thought ominously. Since the day he'd met her she'd never remained far from his thoughts. And with each passing moment she planted herself more firmly in his mind, in his heart.

If his father were behind this, would he be putting her in danger by taking her with him? The question gnawed at him. But the answer remained the same. He knew he shouldn't involve her, but he couldn't stand to be without her. He couldn't leave her — of that, he was certain. She'd be okay; he'd protect her. He would take all precautions to keep her safe.

He had informed Paris of what was going on, and Paris had suggested that Macy not stay in the family villa with him. She would be safer somewhere else. It was better, he figured, if his father thought he was there alone.

They would leave some time tonight and arrive in Palermo in time for his father's weekly meeting with the family. Jordan needed to figure out his strategy. He couldn't just walk in and accuse his father of murder or conspiracy to commit murder. He needed a plan. He lay on his bed trying to think of one, but the one recurring thought was not of his father, nor was it of his dead brother. It was of Macy.

CHAPTER SIX

In the Peach Room Macy re-packed her clothes for the second time in a month cursing Jordan Blake with every movement. That man outraged her, he pissed her off on a daily basis and yet the thought of not being near him had her shivering with queasiness.

She knew the signs, and she knew them well. She was falling for him. God help her, she was falling for her client.

"Hello?" Macy answered the phone that rang on the nightstand beside the bed.

"Macy? A familiar voice addressed her from the other end.

"Steven?" Is that you?" Sitting on the edge of the bed Macy dropped the clothes she held into her suitcase.

"Yeah, it's me. Listen I wanted to talk to you about Blake." He began nervously.

"What about him?" Macy could hear the tense tone of Steven's voice and struggled to remain calm.

"I hear you're going to Sicily with him," he said frankly.

"Yeah, he has some family business to attend to." Macy hesitated a moment. "Steven is there something wrong?" she asked.

"I just, I don't know, I wanted to warn you, to tell you not to go." He was quiet waiting for her response.

"What do you mean warn me?"

"Look, I heard about his brother and I already told you about his father. This was not part of the bargain. Tell him you're coming back to New York. To hell with the firm." Steven yelled into the phone.

Macy knew him well enough to know the signs. He was very angry and she knew why. A year ago, hell a few months ago, she would have been elated. She would have reveled in the turn of events, but now things were different. Jordan had changed them.

"Steven, this is my job. My career. Remember? You were in my office reminding me of that very fact just a few days ago."

"Yeah, but that was before. Before I knew. . ." his voice trailed off as he contemplated telling her.

"Before you knew what?" Tapping her fingernail against the receiver Macy waited for his response.

"Before I knew that he was attracted to you."

"And how is it that you know this now?" Macy asked calmly.

"I just know. No man is going to take you across the country with him and then across the ocean unless he wants to sleep with you. And I'm telling you that's what he plans to do. It's not business for him anymore, its personal." And a part of Steven suffered with that knowledge.

"And what's the problem with that?" Macy asked him. "I'm not attached to anyone and neither is he." Anger slowly began to rise. "Am I supposed to stay alone for the rest of my life? Is that what you want for me?" Raising her voice she questioned the man she once loved.

"Macy don't do this," Steven said quietly. He knew that she had a point. He did want her to be alone. Because she couldn't be with him.

"No, *you* don't do this. What we had was years ago and it ended when you married Anne instead of me. My personal life is my business now, not yours." Tears stung her eyes as she remembered the painful moment when he'd told her of his impending marriage.

"But you have a job to do. You can't do it from Sicily." His temper was rising as well. Macy could hear it in his voice.

"I plan on doing my job. But like I said, what I decide to do with him personally is my business."

"He's dangerous Macy. He'll hurt you." Steven sighed in defeat.

"No more than you did." Her words were icy and cut him quickly.

"I made a mistake," was all he could say.

"Yes you did. But that was your mistake to make. Now let me make my own." Her heart swelled in her chest. The pain of losing Steven still hurt like it was yesterday.

"What about the mafia connection and the danger that goes along with that. You can't tell me that you're willing to risk your life to sleep with this man."

"No, but I will do my best to help a friend."

"You haven't known him long enough to consider him a friend."

"After everything you've done to me I still consider you one." Her voice cracked.

"I'm sorry I hurt you."

"I know."

"I just want you to be safe. I can't wish you happiness, but I can wish for your safety," "Friends wish for each other's happiness too." She smiled lightly.

"Not if it's without me," he said as he realized he was still in love with her.

Macy didn't handle traveling for such long periods of time very well. Just a few days ago, it had been from New York to

Kansas to L.A. And now she was going from L.A. to Sicily. Jet lag was going to be a serious problem. Until this week, the longest she had ever been on a plane had been three hours to Florida. Although she was anxious to see Sicily, she feared she would sleep right through her arrival. Jordan never left her side. Even at their last stopover he was with her while she slept in the airport lobby. She knew she was being a poor traveling companion but she couldn't help it.

Jordan was deathly afraid that Joseph had put too many of those sleeping pills in Macy's coffee. She couldn't seem to stay awake longer than fifteen minutes at a time. And when she was awake it was usually only so that she could use the bathroom.

Jordan had decided that it would be easier if she weren't asking a million questions. He wanted her to believe that the villa she would be staying in belonged to him. He didn't want to have to explain to her why she could not come to his family's estate with him. So, Joseph had given her a few pills to ensure that she remained unaware of her surroundings.

He would return to her at night and sleep at the villa with her when he could, but he did not want anyone to notice that he was away from the main house for fear that they would find out about Macy.

Giving the impression that he was there alone, simply visiting with his father, was very important. As long as no one suspected that he was there to investigate his father's connection to Matthew's death, the easier it would be for him to obtain the information he needed. And until he was absolutely sure that his father was not involved in the murder of his family, he wanted to keep Macy a secret. He could not put her life in danger too; he had already sacrificed her enough by bringing her here; a fact that he buried beneath his desire to be with her.

The pills began to wear off just as they landed. Macy was bound to be groggy but the fresh air on the ferry ride would wake her up. Once off the ferry, there would be another forty-five minute ride to the villa where she would be staying. Paris had once dated the daughter of the caretakers there and he had already spoken with them about the situation, ensuring their silence and cooperation initially.

Aboard the ferry, Macy woke up and looked out into the beautiful open sea. Everyone around her spoke the same language, which she assumed to be Italian. It was beautiful, the words rolled smoothly off their lips like a melody. When they looked her way she simply smiled and prayed they wouldn't start a conversation with her.

"How far is it to your father's house, Jordan?"

"You will be staying at my private villa located at the bottom of Mount Erice. It's surrounded by the sea. I'm sure you'll love it." As he told her, he tucked a wayward strand of hair behind her ears so that he could have an unobstructed view of her face.

"Mount Erice? A villa at the bottom of a mountain? Is that safe?" Macy thought about the volcanoes she had seen on the Discovery Channel.

"It's perfectly safe, Bella. You will be fine there."

"You make it sound like you won't be there with me. I hope you don't think you're going to leave me there alone. You know I don't speak any Italian, Jordan. How will I communicate?" Panic crept into her voice as she wondered about the language barrier.

"Calm down, Macy. I will be there with you when I can. But don't forget my reason for being here. I must see my father and his people so that I can get to the bottom of Matthew's death. I don't want to be here any longer than is absolutely necessary."

"Why not? Don't you like it here?"

"No. I mean the scenery is beautiful, but the memories it evokes aren't. My mother was miserable here with my father and I didn't like seeing my mother miserable. We moved to the States when I was six. Once we got there, my mother seemed to transform into a beautiful flower, like a rose in bloom," Jordan stared out into the ocean as he remembered happier times.

"Why didn't your father come with her?" Macy was curious. Given her curiosity, it was a wonder she hadn't become a journalist. Her thirst for knowledge was insatiable. Either that or she was just plain nosy and wanted to know everything all the time.

"My father was an asshole. His father and his uncles controlled him. He wasn't going to go against anything they told him to do. He met my mother while on a trip to the States, fell in love with her, and asked her father for permission to marry her. With the civil rights movement having just finally gotten off the ground they were a little leery. A rich Italian man marrying a black woman was unheard of. But my grandmother convinced my grandfather that his daughter was in love, and in the end he gave in. The selling point was the fact that they would be living in Sicily. My grandfather desperately wanted a better life for his daughter than what he was giving her in the States. So, my mother left her home, her family and her culture to be with my father." The wind ruffled the inch high hair atop his head. He took a deep breath and continued. "They were married secretly. When they returned to Sicily my father built a special villa for my mother to stay in. He never told his father or his uncles that he was married. He returned to my mother constantly in the beginning, but after she gave birth to two sons, he stopped coming home. Curious, my mother went to my grandfather's home one day and was surprised to see that she had interrupted a wedding. My father was marrying Santina Marcionne. It seems that my grandfather had arranged the marriage when my father and this Santina were young." Continuing to stare into the oblivion of the sea, he paused, wondering if he should continue.

"But how could he marry two women?" Macy asked feeling the sadness of this tragic story.

"His marriage to my mother was never legal, never witnessed by anyone but the old priest they had found to marry them, and he had long since died. Except for his two sons there was no evidence that he even knew Theresa Penelli. Hell, her name was even illegal."

"Then what happened?" Macy watched him intently, entranced by the well of emotions he was revealing.

"My mother ran from the house and began to pack our things. She wanted to return to the States and to her family. The next morning Matthew and I found her lying in a pool of blood with three-inch slits on each of her wrists. Our housekeeper Rosalita was there that morning and she took my mother to the hospital. My father came to see her a few days later. I suspect Rosalita went to him. I often heard her and my mother arguing and Rosalita threatening to go to my father and expose his secret. He told my mother to leave the country, that it was not safe for her here, for she had been spotted at the wedding ceremony and was followed back to her villa that very night. My grandfather had found out about his son's mistress and her children. The next week we came to the States. We never heard from my father again. I believe he sent money in the beginning, but then Mama got a job as a waitress and she took care of us. I have seen my father only once since then," Jordan said sadly.

"At your mother's funeral?" Macy said.

"Yes, he had the nerve to show up at her funeral. I have often wondered how it was that he knew she had died. But I suppose, if he was involved in her murder, of course he would know."

"Is that why you had Matthew cremated?

"Yes, I didn't want a public ceremony and I didn't want my

father to come to the States. I want to confront him on his territory."

"Oh, Jordan, that is so sad. How could he do that to her? How could he do that to his children? I guess it's not just a black thing after all," Macy said pointedly.

"What's not?"

"A man leaving his wife and children for other women. It appears it's universal and multi-cultural," Macy said seriously. "Idiot!" she commented aloud, to herself. Jordan laughed. A rich laugh that was pleasing to Macy's ears.

"I'll be sure to tell him what you think of him, Bella." Macy had never been particularly good at foreign languages, but her assumption was that 'Bella' meant something akin to beauty or some form of feminine praise in Italian. She loved it more each time Jordan said it. His eyes would go soft and he looked at her with such tenderness. Wouldn't it be wonderful to fall in love in Sicily? *Where did that thought come from?* She and Jordan shared a physical attraction for each other, bottom line, *lust*. She had no doubt that they would eventually have sex; it was inevitable. But love was another matter entirely. One which Macy was sure she wasn't ready for.

She was wide-awake during the ride to Pizzolungo. They passed through Ficuzza, a village located just south of Palermo in the township of Corleone. Jordan laughed at Macy's Al Pacino imitation at the mention of Corleone. Most of the way he kept up a steady commentary. He particularly pointed out the lush woods of the nature reserve around Ficuzzo, and when they passed the Villa Trabia, he mentioned that it was one of the few aristocratic homes open to the public. Built for the Prince of Trabia in the eighteenth century, its coat of arms gleamed in the morning sunlight and flowers hung from the balconies.

They continued to travel along the coast, stopping briefly at Mondello Beach on the western side of Mount Pellegrino where they had lunch at an excellent seafood restaurant, then toured a few of the medieval watchtowers before continuing to Mount Erice.

Pizzolungo was magnificent. Macy especially liked the Pepoli Castle and Venus Castle and would have been satisfied had her trip to Sicily stopped right there. But they traveled on until they came to their destination.

Surprisingly, there was an enormous vegetable garden right in the middle of the villa's courtyard. According to Jordan the caretakers sold the vegetables as well as wine and olive oil to keep up the maintenance on the villa when tourism was down in the winter months.

Macy was led to a small cottage at the far end of the main house. When she stepped inside, she was astounded by its attractiveness. Bigger than her apartment back in New York, it had a large living/dining room with two sleep sofas, a kitchenette, a double bedroom and a roomy bathroom with shower. At the far end of the bedroom there was a window seat much like the one in the Peach Room at Jordan's house in L.A., though it wasn't as luxurious.

She quickly began to unpack, anxious to go out and look around. Though she had gotten her passport when she turned eighteen just so she would have it ready when she was finally able to travel, this was her first overseas trip and she intended to make the most of it.

"Macy, I have to go see my father now," Jordan said from the doorway.

"You're not going to give me the grand tour?" Macy was so wrapped up in the beauty of Sicily and the aura of romance in the air that she was disappointed that Jordan would leave her so soon after their arrival. Of course, she knew his purpose in coming to

Sicily wasn't to fall in love, or to cater to some fantasy that existed only in her imagination. Still, she wanted to be with him. And for that, she could kick herself.

She was supposed to be working. His case was important both to the firm and to her. She really needed to pull those contracts out of her travel bag and go over them with a fine tooth comb. She was sure there was something in there that would aid in Jordan's defense. Some small loop hole always existed. You just had to know how to find it.

When Jordan didn't answer she turned to find out why. She followed his mesmerized gaze to her open suitcase. A lacy pink satin nightgown lay on top.

He stood perfectly still as visions of Macy wearing this garment danced through his head. Thoroughly embarrassed, she quickly grabbed the garment and stuffed it into the drawer.

"Sorry," she said shyly.

"No need to apologize. Seeing that just brought forth images that I have been trying to restrain."

"What types of images?" *Stupid, stupid question, Macy.*

"I imagined us on that big bed, you wearing only that nightgown, me wearing nothing. Our bodies coming together, entwining until we become one. Our pleasure producing a symphony of moans and indistinguishable murmurs of delight. Me kissing you all over and you whimpering my name. Oh Bella, you can see it too, can't you?" Standing in the doorway with his eyes half closed he allowed the images to be permanently implanted in his memory.

Macy, overwhelmed, took the only route she knew. Defense.

"Here we go again. First, you pull strings on my job, and then you fly me across the ocean. Now you apparently expect me to throw myself in that bed and let you do all those things to me. I don't know what type of women you're used to dealing with, but I assure you, Mr. Blake, that I am not interested in you or your misguided assessment of what we would be like in bed together," Macy's tone was vehement. But despite herself she envisioned them lying there together and all the things they would undoubtedly do. She turned away lest his dark eyes see the truth. A truth, she herself, didn't yet want to acknowledge.

"Macy, my dear sweet Macy. I don't know why you insist on fighting the inevitable. It's fate that we've ended up together and because of that our happiness has been insured. I only wish to hurry things along a bit." Closing the distance between them, he lightly traced her bottom lip with his thumb. Instinctively her tongue retraced the spot seconds after he removed his finger. Bending his head, he gently touched his lips to hers. Macy could feel the room revolving around her.

"I will have you Macy," he whispered against her lips. "It's just a matter of time. Your body betrays your mind. I feel it every time I touch you. Just let me love you." Cutting off the outraged response he knew she was formulating in that beautiful head of hers, he kissed her.

His words vibrated in her head and she knew that his reference to love was of a purely sexual nature. So what was wrong with that? Maybe nothing. But she couldn't examine the words or their true meaning right now. She could only think of one thing at that moment. Jordan.

Returning his kiss with vigor and aggression to match his, she lost herself in his touch. If this were all she could have, she'd gladly take it, for now.

Jordan reluctantly pulled away. "I'll be back in time for dinner. Will you wait for me?"

"Yes. I'll be waiting." And she knew that she would.

She sounded so sexy and looked so good Jordan had to force

himself to turn and leave the room.

After that episode Macy needed a cool shower. Once that was out of the way, she set out on her adventure, needing to keep herself busy so that Jordan would be the farthest thing from her mind. Immediately upon leaving the cottage she met a couple from the cottage next to hers.

They introduced themselves as Alice and Antonio Masseretti and said something about Switzerland. Their English was choppy at best and Macy knew absolutely no Italian or whatever language it was that they were speaking. She assumed they were vacationers from Switzerland. Oddly enough, Mr. Masseretti looked familiar. She chalked it up to her jet lag and continued her stroll. Stopping at the massive garden she pondered her feelings for Jordan Blake.

She had never been one to believe in love at first sight or overnight romances, but that seemed to be exactly what she was experiencing with Jordan. She had known him little more than a week and he was already changing her. That angered her. How could she so easily forfeit the plans she had made for herself? She knew she'd never be able to be a partner at the firm if she were with him; he'd distract her, just as he was doing now. Just look at her! She hadn't done any legal work since she'd been with him other than read a few contracts and make a few phone calls. On the other hand, the lawyer in her agreed that there were plenty of women who had successful relationships and thriving careers. If they could do it, she was almost positive that she could too. But hadn't she thought the same thing before and failed.

Thoughts of the fifteen months she had been involved with Steven came rushing back into her mind. She'd tried to balance the job and her life with him and she'd failed dismally. Steven had wanted a wife and kids, but Macy had been reluctant. She'd wanted her feet planted firmly in her career before she gave the family thing a shot. And in the end Steven had found what he needed elsewhere.

Accepting the blame for the demise of that relationship had helped Macy and Steven remain good friends. He needed to move on, she had told herself, and so did she. But where did that leave her now? Was she about to make the same choice she'd made then?

Clearing her head, she tried to focus on the here and now. What had happened before was over, and there was nothing she could do to change it. But she vowed not to make the same mistake twice. If she wanted Jordan, and she now admitted to herself that she did, then she'd have to do whatever was necessary to get him on her terms.

Of course, Jordan would have to stop being so bossy all the time, but she could get around that if she could just get him to have some real feelings for her. She wondered how she could convince him that she was worth more than a quick roll in the sack? She was almost positive that was all he was looking for, though the way he looked at her at times and the way he called her '*Bella*' almost had her imagining that he was developing deeper feelings of his own. But she figured those feelings stopped just below the belt.

In truth, this man was driving her crazy. One minute she detested him and what he was doing to her and the next she was plotting how to make him want her more. She was definitely losing it. Accepting that Jordan was thoroughly confusing her, she figured she'd dish out some confusion of her own.

The way to a man's heart is through his stomach. She had heard that on lots of those old movies she watched when she couldn't sleep at night. Picking a tomato from the long vines that ran through the garden, she decided that she'd cook him something, maybe flirt a little and see just what Mr. Arrogant did when the tables were turned.

"*Senorita, pomodori, si,*" An elderly woman, who seemed to

come from nowhere, said to Macy.

"I'm sorry, I don't speak Italian." Macy felt a little alarmed and confused.

"You eat *pomodori*? How do you say . . . tomatoes?" The old woman pointed to the tomato Macy held in her hand.

"Yes, I want to prepare a meal for my friend."

"*Senor* Jordan? He like tomatoes. I help you, *si*?" The woman picked more tomatoes and some leafy looking things.

"What's your name?" Macy asked as the old woman continued to stuff things from the garden into a basket she held on her arm.

"*Ti*, Rosalita. You *senorita*, are Macy. *Senor* Jordan tell me to take good care of you." Macy laughed. That sounded just like something Jordan would say. *Rosalita, this must be the housekeeper Jordan's mother had had. Which meant she knew Jordan very well.*

"Rosalita, I was thinking of preparing a meal for *Senor* Jordan. What else does he like?"

"*Nocino. Ti*, I show you how to make. Must hurry. *Senor* be home soon. Lots to do." Rosalita stood about five feet tall and was as round as a bouncing ball. She cheerfully ran about the garden picking and snapping things from the voluminous plants. Occasionally she would turn to Macy and motion for her to do the same. She chatted incessantly in Italian. Macy was going to have to get a book or something; this language thing was rattling her nerves.

From a balcony on the second story of the main house the man watched Macy, mentally familiarizing himself with her. He wasn't sure of her connection to his plan, but he had decided to keep her in sight. In the meantime, he could use a few days of relaxation. That guy in Vegas had put up one hell of a fight. But everything had gone according to schedule, and now he was ready for the last stage of his plan.

He hadn't anticipated that Jordan would come back to Sicily. He had really wanted to wrap this up in the States, but Jordan was a sharp one. Even after the death of his mother, Jordan had been suspicious. But none of that mattered now. Time was winding down and things were coming full circle. Jordan was going to get the answers that he was in search of, but when he did it would be too late to do anything about it.

He walked back into his room, to wait. Time was winding down and he was anxious to get it over with.

CHAPTER SEVEN

Over seventy miles away Jordan wasn't having as good an afternoon as Macy and Rosalita. Maria, one of the maids at Villa Santiaga, his father's estate, was being very tightlipped about her boss's whereabouts. When Jordan informed her that he was Dioncello's eldest son, she, like many other people, had trouble believing him. His dark complexion caused hesitation, even though it had been rumored through the town for years that Dioncello had once taken a black woman. Maria finally told him that Dioncello and his wife were in Naples visiting her sick mother. Because this, in all likelihood, would be their last visit with her they would be staying a while. Jordan's inquiries about social comings and goings and visitors to the estate went unanswered. His father had trained her well. She would not be giving up any family secrets today, or any other day for that matter.

Jordan walked the busy streets leading back to the road where his car waited to take him back to Pizzolungo. People were everywhere. They seemed to be gathered around talking and laughing rather than working. At the sight of the stranger in town, however, their voices were lowered to hushed tones. Seeing this, Jordan decided that he would need to enlist someone to help him in his investigation. He was a stranger to them both in looks and in culture. They did not know him to be Dioncello's son, and he wasn't sure he wanted them to.

In the years since his mother moved him and his younger

brother to the States, Jordan had returned to Sicily only twice. And on neither occasion had he visited Villa Santiaga because he didn't want to communicate with the man who had caused his mother such hurt and disgrace. His brother Matthew, on the other hand, forgave his father and had even stayed with him for about a year after he graduated from college. According to Matthew, their father had been very civil to him, even fatherly at times. So what motive could Dioncello have for Matthew's murder?

Unless it wasn't his father personally who wanted Matthew murdered but someone connected to his father in some way. Maybe even someone his father had pissed off. There was that rumor that his father was involved with the Mafia. Somehow, some way, Jordan intended to get to the bottom of Matthew's murder.

But not now. Now his intention was to get back to Macy. It was hard to concentrate on the matter at hand when he knew she was back at the cottage waiting for him to return. He had been attracted to her from the start, but in the days that he'd been with her, something that passed physical attraction seemed to be happening. He liked her, not only the way she looked, but the way she argued with him. That was something. He had never had a woman argue with him the way Macy did. This intrigued him, hell; it turned him on even more. He needed to get back to her.

Macy covered every detail to create a sensual mood. They would dine by candlelight. With Rosalita's help, she had prepared a dinner of Italian dishes: caponata, a salad made with eggplant, capers, olives and celery, and schiaffi, a type of ravioli. They would drink nocino wine and for dessert dine on mantovana, a torte made with almonds and walnuts. According to Rosalita, all these things were Jordan's favorites. And that was all that mattered to Macy, so she had paid scant attention to Rosalita's ramblings about the ingredients and preparation. It was enough that Jordan liked everything.

After Rosalita's departure Macy took a long hot bath and massaged a floral scented oil that Rosalita had given her into her skin as she'd instructed. Thinking a casual outfit would entice Jordan, she dressed in simple black slacks and a button-down, pink cotton shirt. That covered the casual. For the really enticing, she wore thong panties that were a whisper of black lace and a matching bra – items she had somewhat cynically thrown into her luggage at the last minute.

She calmly wandered back into the kitchen where she had set the table, checking and double-checking to make sure everything was just right. Everything was perfect. The food smelled wonderfully. She looked nice. She was calm, cool and collected, for now. When Jordan returned it might be a completely different story.

He came into the cottage hot and sweaty but starving for the sight of Macy. Although, it was a seasonal seventy-six degrees, it felt like an L.A. scorcher. He'd spent the day walking the streets of Palermo, and the shirt he wore was sticking to his chest. He needed a shower in the worst way. Despite that, he smelled roses the minute he walked in. Then he noticed the candles and the elegantly set table.

"Hey, I thought you'd never get here." Macy appeared from the bedroom. Jordan's pulse quickened, and a throbbing began between his legs. It took everything he had in him to speak with a calm voice.

"Shall I take that to mean that you missed me?"

"That depends." Macy walked toward him, the gentle sway in her hips making him shift to hide his growing erection.

"On what?"

"On how much you . . . you . . . you smell awful, Jordan. Where have you been?" Holding her hand to her nose, Macy backed away. He was giving a new meaning to hot and sweaty; his musty aroma was not enticing in the least bit.

"It gets pretty hot in the city. I'll just get a quick shower and I'll be right back,"

He showered in record time. His body ached to be near her, to touch her. She was driving him crazy.

Macy was very nervous about the evening and was anxious to get things rolling. "Jordan!" she called out to him. "Are you almost finished? The food is ready and..." she stopped abruptly as she saw him standing in the entryway.

Noting her surprise, Jordan came in and sat opposite her at the table. How did she expect him to eat when her breasts were all but falling out of that shirt? Food was the last thing on his mind. Nevertheless, he would not make a fool of himself. This was not his first encounter with a woman. But Macy was not just any woman. She was *the* woman. He knew that and was as sure as the days were long that she would always be *the* woman for him.

As a teenager he had asked his mother why she had never remarried. She had looked at him seriously and said, "You will have only one true love, Jordan. When you find it, hold on to it for it will never come again." Jordan intended to do just that.

"Why did you braid your hair?" He said after about five minutes of staring at her. She had pulled her hair back into a loose French braid and secured it with an allotment of hairpins that she made a point never to travel without.

"You don't like it?" she asked just a little too nicely.

"I like it down, but it's fine like that too," Jordan said hurriedly. He had detected the edge in her voice despite her smiling face. The last thing he wanted was to make her angry.

Macy linked her fingers into the bottom of the braid and pulled it free. The wavy mass of hair lay loosely at her shoulders. She continued to swipe at it, hoping that it wasn't sticking straight in the air.

"I aim to please," she said.

Jordan was on her side of the table instantly, lifting her from her chair and carrying her into the bedroom.

"Jordan, we haven't eaten yet!"

"I have what I want right here." Stopping just short of the bed, he stood her before him, his eyes intent on hers. She could see the deep passion burning within him. She wanted to share that with him; she wanted it so bad she could almost taste it. Her breasts ached for him to touch her, to make her his.

"Jordan, maybe we should talk about this first." She heard the words but she didn't take the suggestion any more seriously than he had. Talking was out of the question now; Jordan's fingers quickly unbuttoning her shirt had answered that.

"The only talking I'll be doing is describing what I intend to do to you." Discarding her shirt he placed an open palm on her chest and watched its quick rise and fall as her breathing intensified.

"Are you afraid, *Bella*?" Macy shook her head, 'no'. She couldn't speak. Couldn't put into words what his closeness was doing to her.

"Watch me, *Bella*. Look straight into my eyes." Macy did as she was told. Slipping his fingers beneath thin straps of black material, he removed her bra and looked at her breasts. Her breasts tumbled free from the material. Her nipples tingled from their erectness. His tongue caressed each one giving them all his attention. When Macy lifted her hands to run them through his hair, he felt a sudden relief overcome him. She did want him and she wanted what he was doing to her.

Jordan's throat grew dry. Could he handle doing this slowly? Yes, he could, and he would because Macy deserved it. He knelt before trailing feather-like kisses down her stomach. He could smell roses. His tongue stroked her skin tenderly; he could feel her struggling for control.

"Macy, are you with me?" he asked.

"Yes . . . Jordan, I'm with you." She looked at him with such honesty, such trust. He wanted to give her the world. His hands cupped her breasts again, molding them to fit his palms.

Macy couldn't contain her own passion any longer. She let out a small cry, arching her back and giving him full access.

"Jordan." No other man had ever come close to awakening the feelings that he had. She knew there would never be another.

"*Bella*, my sweet *Bella*. Tell me what you want."

"I want you to touch me, Jordan," Macy gasped.

He lowered her to the bed hesitating briefly before joining her. Reaching out to touch him she sighed, "Jordan."

She said his name again as his lips met hers, devouring her. His tongue boldly claiming her as his own, he mastered her mouth and body until she wanted to scream. He unbuttoned her pants and pulled them down her strong legs. Gently he brushed feather-like kisses over her ankles before taking each one of her toes and sucking lightly. Progressing north he kissed the back of her legs. "Wider." He whispered, nudging her thighs further apart. He tasted the smooth softness of the skin of her inner thigh before rubbing one finger down the center of her.

Macy could never have anticipated the fire Jordan's tongue would ignite when it touched that sacred place. Jordan almost yelled at the sweetness of her nectar.

"Oh, Jordan," was all she could manage before she was lost in the oblivion of her own pleasure. When he left her to take his clothes off, it occurred to her that she was doing a poor job of making him fall in love with her. Up until now she had been on the receiving end of all the pleasure. It was time to take a little control. She reared up on the bed in time to see him dropping his boxers to the floor. He was glorious naked -like a Greek god with curves and muscle bulging from everywhere. His skin was the color of a bronze statue; hard muscles and sharp angles had her catching her breath.

"Are you okay?" Jordan asked, wondering if he displeased her.

"I'm just wondering how long it's gonna take you to get over here." Jordan laughed and climbed into bed next to her.

"You know, if you're not sure we can stop." Jordan eyed her as he waited for her answer, his hands pushing the rowdy waves of her hair away from her face.

"Are you kidding? Since the day I met you you've made no secret of the fact that you wanted me in bed and now that you have me here you're trying to back down. Well, you can just forget it, mister. You're in for the long haul," She climbed on top of him.

Briefly shocked, Jordan adjusted himself to the change in command and anxiously anticipated her next move.

Macy lowered her head to nip his lip but he caught the back of her neck and held her there to begin another brutal assault on her mouth. They kissed until his probing sex almost made its entrance without verbal consent. Macy reached between their bodies, wrapping her fingers around the swollen organ. Jordan sucked in air and it seemed that he held it in until Macy's tongue exchanged positions with her hands and it exploded from him. Her tongue caressed and massaged as Jordan began the timeless motion of his hips.

Unable to wait another moment he swiftly entered her, holding her perfectly still for the first agonizing moments as the slickness of her almost drowned him.

Then she began to ride, taking him to a place he'd never been before. She moved with accurate quickness, and then slowed to a mellow torture.

"*Ti ador, angelo mio. Getterò petali di rosa ai tuoi piedi. Come sei Bella. Come sei Bella*." Jordan repeated over and over again. The smooth sound of the Italian language coming from him only heightened Macy's fervor. Jordan gloried in the sight of her atop him. Her mane of black hair framed her small delicate face, and amber eyes held a soft sheen of pure pleasure. He was nearing his release and he knew that Macy was soon to follow.

"Look at me, *Bella*," he demanded. She opened her eyes to stare at him. "You are mine now," he said as he stared at her fiercely. Macy nodded in compliance.

"Say it *Bella*. Say that you're mine," he repeated through clenched teeth.

"I am yours, Jordan. I am yours." With her confession came their release.

Sometime in the late evening when the only sound in the room was the low hum of contented breath a thought occurred to Jordan. He hadn't used any protection and they hadn't discussed any. He had planned on it, he really had. The proof lay in the back pocket of the pants he wore and in the inner zipper of his suitcase.

But she had taken him by storm. The wanting he had been banking for so long had overtaken him. He wondered how she would react when he brought it up.

"What are you thinking so hard about?" Macy asked at the site of the frown lines in his forehead.

"I was just remembering. . ." he hesitated briefly. "You know we forgot something." Cutting his eyes at her he hoped she would understand his meaning without him actually having to say it. And after a few seconds she did.

"Oh!" Bringing her hand to cover her mouth she sat up in the bed. "We did, didn't we?" She'd known this man less than a month and she slept with him unprotected. She almost cringed at the thought, then relaxed as she felt his hands on her shoulders.

"I apologize, it was my fault." Accepting the blame he pulled her back to lie across his broad chest. "It won't happen again," He vowed.

"It wasn't only your fault. I'm a big girl; I know the risks too. I should have said something," she admitted.

A few tense moments passed before Jordan rose from the bed pulling her with him. "Let's eat I'm starving."

Giggling, Macy pulled at the sheet in an effort to cover herself.

"It's a little late for that don't you think?" Taking the wrinkled sheet from her Jordan threw it back onto the bed. "Besides, I like you better this way." He quickly bent over to kiss a blooming nipple before pulling her toward the door.

Her romantic dinner had managed to shift the almost somber mood their slip up had caused. They enjoyed it, in bed of course.

"You cooked this yourself, *Bella*?" Jordan asked as he sipped on his nocino.

"Yes. Well, almost. I met Rosalita. She helped me,"

"Rosalita's a great cook but I'm sure she didn't give away all her secrets."

"She said she would tell me everything *Senor* Jordan liked." As she sat up to do her Rosalita impression the sheet fell, revealing one honey-toned breast. There was no more conversation.

Standing at the open window where he had witnessed a couple's mating, the man attempted to clean the mess the erotic scene had evoked. He had gotten a little carried away in his stakeout. He had been thrilled to find out that Jordan had a girlfriend and ecstatic when he saw her with him tonight. She was extraordinary when fully clothed and simply awesome when naked. Seeing Macy pleasuring Jordan had given him a whole new outlook on the previously planned revenge. How better to start the process of destroying Jordan Blake than by having his woman. He'd have to make some alterations to the original plan but it would be worth it.

CHAPTER EIGHT

After their first week there Jordan finally gave in to Macy's requests for a tour of the city. He still didn't think that it was safe for them to be seen outside of Pizzolungo together but he couldn't continue to turn her down.

He wanted to do something special for her so he planned a day of sight seeing with Tony, a friend of Rosalita. He would take them to see the sights in the city as he delivered the vegetables and fruits his parents grew and sold.

Dressed for the occasion, Macy had never looked more beautiful. She wore a yellow sundress and yellow sandals that laced midway up her calves. Her hair was pulled back into a loose ponytail and tied with a yellow and red silk scarf that hung in a loose bow. She was exquisite. His Macy. That's how he thought of her.

"Come on, Jordan, quit your dilly-dallying or we'll miss him. He had dressed in tan khaki shorts with a red polo shirt but barely had time to put on his sandals before she was pulling him out to the cart. His assurance that Tony would not leave them counted for nothing.

"*Bella*, he is not going to leave us," he repeated. "I promise." He stooped to fasten his sandals. When he stood he looked into those gorgeous eyes and saw how truly happy she was. "Okay. Let's go,"

They traveled south along the coast. Macy took in everything. She didn't ask as many questions as he had anticipated, but then they were still in the area that Rosalita had prepped her on. As they rode along quietly, Macy's thoughts turned to the investigation.

"How's your investigation coming, Jordan?" she asked suddenly. He hadn't volunteered any information.

"Slowly. I don't have any real leads, and my father and his wife are away."

"Are you positive that your father is involved? I mean, what if you're just jumping to conclusions."

"No, I'm not positive, but I have a really strong feeling that he is. Why are you asking?"

"No reason. I'm just concerned," She fell silent.

"Come on, *Bella*, what are you thinking? Don't tell me *nothing*," he turned in the seat so that he faced her.

"I just think that you might be wrong. I mean, why would a father want to hurt his own children? I know about the situation with him and your mother, but that was between them. His children had nothing to do with that,"

"Well, if you think he was so concerned about his children, then why did he choose to send us away and never visit?" Jordan asked.

"I don't know, Jordan, and neither do you. So don't you think you owe him a chance to explain that before you accuse him of murder? I mean, there may be things that your mother didn't tell you, you know, extenuating circumstances. You have heard of extenuating circumstances, haven't you?" Macy lifted her chin to feel the slight breeze that passed through the trees. She didn't understand his feelings towards his father. Maybe because she grew up with both her parents, she couldn't relate to one parent not wanting to be with her.

George F. Glenn had been a wonderful man. A powerful attorney who had gone on to become an effective congressman. His career came second only to his family. Her parents had shared a love that she'd envied; a friendship that she longed for. Their marriage had been what she'd wanted when she grew up.

And he'd loved his daughters just as fiercely, protecting and nurturing them along the way. So when he suddenly collapsed in his office, her family had been devastated. A massive heart attack, the doctor had told them when they'd arrived at the hospital. Her mother had crumbled, and she and her sister had wept.

Her father lay in that bed surrounded by white sheets and noisy machinery. His once strong jaw slack with the pain that had riddled through him. The hands that had held hers so many times before lay quietly beside him. The warm brown eyes that normally danced with happiness were closed and with them all joy for the Glenn family was too.

He struggled for a few hours, and then he was gone. So quick, so sudden, so final. Macy had never suffered anything so devastating in her life and she hoped she'd never have to again.

"Look, I know that this may all seem strange to you but I have lived with it all my life. I have survived knowing that my father would rather have another woman instead of my mother and his children. And up until my mother's death I had gotten over the disappointment of not being good enough for him. But I can't ignore the fact that he might be connected or at least know something. As for my personal feelings for him, well, I have none anymore. He is just another man to me. So no, it's too late for me to consider any 'extenuating circumstances' as you put it. At this stage of the game I don't even care about what happened between him and my mother. I just want to know who killed her and Matthew. And I'm sorry if you can't understand that."

Macy could see that she had upset him, and that was the last thing she'd wanted to do. But she also didn't want him to pass up an opportunity to get to know his father better, by letting past mistakes, albeit very big past mistakes, get in the way of that. She knew that he held a lot of resentment towards his father, and while she couldn't say that she blamed him, she also could see that he needed to know him. He needed to know who his father really was because he was a part of him and the man he had become. But now was not the time to pursue that issue with him.

"I'm sorry, Jordan. I just want you to know what I think. I won't ask you about it again," She placed her hand in his, and he lifted her fingers to his mouth, kissing each one.

"There is nothing for you to be sorry about, *Bella*. You didn't make this situation what it is. And I don't want you to ever feel that you can't tell me what you think, no matter what it is. Agreed?"

"Agreed." She smiled as she waited for the familiar feel of his mouth on hers.

They approached the city as it neared lunchtime. Tony had pointed out a nice little restaurant in a town called Santo Stefano Quisquina, located in the Province of Agrigento.

They finished the meal with Sicilian gelato. Macy and Jordan shared a beautifully pink fragala flavor that Jordan insisted on feeding to Macy spoonful by delicious spoonful. According to the waiter, the ice cream was invented in Sicily during Roman times. He charmed Macy with his story of runners bringing snow down from Mount Etna to be flavored and served to wealthy patricians.

As they waited for Tony to finish with his customers Jordan enjoyed a conversation with the owner of the restaurant.

"Well, Ms. Macy, it seems as though we picked the perfect day to go sight seeing," Jordan announced as he returned to sit next to her at their table.

"Why do you say that?"

"Apparently we are just in time for the Feast of Santa Rosalia,"

"What's that? It sounds like fun."

Anything that concerned food sounded like fun to Macy. Jordan had learned that she had a healthy appetite; he was amazed that she could stay so thin, but then she rarely sat still long enough to gain weight.

"What's what? The feast or the woman?" he teased.

"Both, Jordan."

"Okay, Santa Rosalia, or La Santuzza, which means "the little saint," was the daughter of Duke Sinibaldo, Lord of the Quisquina and the Roses, who was a cousin of King William II of Sicily. Rosalia had chosen to lead a life of solitude and devoted herself to prayer." His voice was so rich and so soothing as he told the old story. Macy was entranced.

"Oh, like Saint Francis of Assisi," she said. She had learned about him in a history course she had taken in college.

"Yeah, just like him. The legend says that in 1159 she retired and resumed a hermit-like existence in a cave on Monte Pellegrino. Nothing was heard from her until 1624 when the plague arrived in Sicily. Santa Rosalia appeared in a vision to a hunter lost on Monte Pellegrino. She told him not to worry, that she would protect him and the city. She revealed to him the site of the cave where she had lived and told him to go back to Palermo and alert the archbishop and rulers of the city. The hunter did as he was told, and those leaders found her remains and displayed them through the streets of Palermo.

Within three days, the plague ended, and she was proclaimed patron saint of the city. So the first week of June every year the people of Santo Stefano Quisquina, where we are at this very moment, have a special celebration to commemorate her intervention that saved Palermo from the Black Plague,"

"Oh, my. I'm glad we came today. When does the feast begin?"

Macy asked, thinking of what foods she could enjoy this time.

"The feast usually doesn't take place until after sunset. First they have the processional through the hills of Mt. Quisquina, then a horseback processional through the city. And since we've already missed the processional, why don't we visit the statue of Santa Rosalia?" He stood and took her hand. She was more than eager to accompany him.

They traveled through winding roads and woods of typically Mediterranean stone pines to where the statue stood amidst glorious flowers and large intricately designed columns. The beautiful sight almost brought Macy to tears. Then they followed the main road past the sanctuary to the mountain's summit where they marveled at the view of Mondello and the Sea.

"Jordan this is so beautiful. I mean, it's . . . its beyond beautiful, it's breathtaking," Macy said as they stood with the wind lightly brushing against their skin.

"Yeah, it is. I've never been to this point myself. I'm glad I'm sharing it with you," he spoke seriously and turned Macy to face him.

"I'm glad you are too." Small curls of his jet-black hair twisted in the wind and the sun reflected in his dark eyes. But today she could see tenderness in those eyes, a slight softening. She reached out to cup his face and he quickly turned her hand to kiss her palm. A familiar throbbing in his pelvis suddenly had Jordan shifting uncomfortably.

"Maybe we should head back," he said. He turned to guide Macy down the path.

"Okay," Macy struggled to stifle a smile. She'd felt Jordan's arousal and was pleased.

Once back at the cart Tony took them into Palermo.

The Marionette Museum near the water at the end of Corso

Vittorio Emanuele held an extensive collection of Sicilian puppets, some centuries old, some dating back to the Sicilian *"opera di pupi"* or puppet opera.

Next on Tony's tour came the Cathedral of Palermo. The varied styles of architecture that had been used in the creation of the cathedral amazed Macy. In the chapel, she stared in awe at the relics and the gold tiara on display.

"You know, when I was little, before we left Sicily, I dreamt that one day I would meet a beautiful woman and we would marry right here in this church," Jordan said absently. Then as if he remembered that Macy stood next to him, he quickly hurried her out of the church and into the streets once again. He had been hurrying her about all afternoon, but now she noticed that he had begun looking over his shoulder and paying attention to every little thing that was going on around them. She began to worry. Did he think someone was following them? Rather than risk getting him upset again and spoiling their day, she decided not to mention it. They continued in silence for a while longer until Jordan abruptly steered them to a cart on one of the side streets. He began a conversation in Italian with the woman who worked the cart as Macy casually surveyed the pedestrians and buildings.

A couple arguing in front of a particularly odd-looking building suddenly caught her attention. The woman began to cry. Macy gasped when the man slapped her. As if he heard her, he looked up and locked gazes with Macy. She couldn't swear to it but the man and woman looked like Mr. and Mrs. Masseretti.

"What's the matter?"

She jumped as she heard Jordan's voice. "What? Oh, nothing. I was just looking around," she lied.

"I got you something," he handed her the bundle of flowers he had purchased from the woman at the cart.

"Oh, Jordan, they're so pretty. Thank you," She stood on tiptoe to kiss him. She had meant for it to be only a light kiss, but he turned it into something different. While it wasn't a deep passionate kiss, the touch of his tongue to hers ignited a fire in her that she couldn't explain. As she stepped back to look at him, she could see that he had felt the same thing.

They rode home in silence. Not a deafening silence, but an intimate silence as they both anticipated what was to come. Jordan was so engrossed in his thoughts of Macy that he failed to notice a cart that had remained on the same road with them throughout their ride back to Pizzolungo.

Two more weeks passed and Macy was getting bored. She pondered her situation as she strolled a path near the cottage. She loved being with Jordan but she missed New York. She missed doing business. Sure, Sicily was lovely and she and Rosalita took long walks every day, and the Mediterranean was indeed beautiful, but none of this compared to the hustle and bustle of New York. She needed confrontation, business lunches, dinner parties and cocktails. For her, it was time to go. She wasn't sure if Jordan was any closer to finding his family's killers. She hadn't dared to broach the subject again. Besides, when they were together they usually were too busy making love to talk. Whenever they did talk, it was about their future. Their business future. Jordan gave Macy more of the specifics of the lawsuit, along with an account of all the business dealings he had going on at the moment. Macy was disappointed at his businesslike manner. She had thought they were getting closer and that they shared something important together, but anytime they weren't in bed he treated her like an assistant. A highly favored assistant, she might add, but an assistant nonetheless.

She smiled as she remembered the day back in New York when she had told him that their relationship would remain professional or she'd quit. Oh, how that had changed.

She remembered the night they'd returned to the cottage after their day of sight seeing. The room had been quiet, the wine had been chilled and the bath had been drawn. Walking into the floral scented bathroom Macy smiled. "Rosalita," she said, more of a whisper than a pronouncement.

Jordan had entered the bathroom behind her gently wrapping his arm around her waist. "Someone has read my mind." Placing feather-like kisses down the back of her neck he felt Macy's pulse quicken.

Eyeing the bathtub that had been filled with pink and red rose petals and the candles that seemed to give off their own distinctive smell Macy relaxed into his embrace. "I should say so." Cradling her head on his shoulder, she allowed him greater access to her neck.

"I don't know what you're doing to me, *Bella.*" Jordan whispered between kisses. His tongue warming each spot it sought.

"The same thing you're doing to me." Turning to face him her arms wrapped around his neck pulling him to her. Taking his mouth hungrily Macy stood on tiptoe to deepen the contact.

Deft hands removed her clothes and she stood before him naked. His disrobing was considerably slower, at Macy's request. His muscles tensed and became more rigid as her fingers explored their contours.

He was hard and strong . . . and hers, she thought to herself. This man who had barged into her life, had somehow managed to embed himself into her soul. Her lips touched the smooth skin of his chest and moved to one hardened pebble.

On a low groan, he gently placed her in the tub. The water was hot, startling initially, then soothing muscles that had been stressed during the day. Climbing in behind her he cradled her between his legs. She lay back onto his chest while his large melodious hands kneaded her breasts.

Rose petals floated in the water, grazing their skin, both texture and scent arousing them. No words were spoken. None were needed.

Her hands passed over taut thigh muscles as she felt his hardness growing at her back. He nipped her earlobe. Inaudible mumbling came from his mouth. Lifting a sponge he squeezed it firmly above her breasts. Hot water streamed down over the swollen mounds.

She released a small gasp at the sensations that coursed through her. Never had she experienced something so simple, yet so erotic.

"*Il letto*." He breathed harshly.

"What's that?" she asked, not, bothering to open her eyes.

"It means the bed." He chuckled and she stirred at the rumbling in his chest. "I think we should start your first lesson in Italiano tonight." He suggested.

"Now?" Lifting from his chest she questioned his timing.

"Now." Standing, he stepped out of the tub. Turning to take her hands in his he helped her out.

She stared up at him questioningly. "Trust me." He smiled.

She did, so she followed him into the bedroom without further hesitation. The soft comforter that adorned the bed had been turned down, the pillows tilted and puffed to perfection. With the towel he had brought from the bathroom he began to gently pat at her skin, dropping kisses here and there.

A.C. ARTHUR

Quickly, roughly, he dragged the same towel over himself before tossing it to the floor and placing her on the bed.

"Lesson one, parts of the body." He hovered above her reveling in her beauty.

"Shall I take notes?" A smile teased lips already swollen from his previous attention.

"I don't think you'll have any problems remembering what I'm about to teach you." He took her mouth then, plunging deeply and leaving her limp.

"*Il collo*." He kissed her neck. "*Il petto*." He kissed her chest. "*L'anca*." He paused and his tongue lavished the skin on her hip.

"Jordan." His name escaped her lips. His blood pumped faster.

"*La gamba*." Feather-like kisses rained down first one leg, and then the other. "*Il piede*." Holding one small foot in his hand, his tongue tracing a line from her ankle to the base of her toes. "*Il ditto del piede*." Taking one vulnerable toe into his mouth, he suckled.

Macy squirmed, shaking her head against the pillows, against the waves of pleasure that were thrashing within her. She was lost in his voice that was like a sweet melody washing over her, husky and aroused.

Returning to lay beside her at the top of the bed, he pulled her so that she straddled him. Lifting one hand he cupped her breast softly, "*Seno*." His eyes were clouded, passion filling him completely.

"*Bellisimo*." He whispered as his attentions turned to the other breast. "Beautiful."

Sliding his hand between her legs he found her bud, puckered and wet. She arched above him barely restraining her pleasure.

His ministrations were driving her mad. Had she known learning Italian was going to be like this she would have gladly taken it in college.

Grabbing her hips he positioned her above his throbbing sex. Guiding her slowly he let himself fill her. She let herself surround him.

Moving together, soaring together their hands clasped, their minds free. The release was quick, shattering everything inside her; consuming all that he was.

She lay beside him, her legs entwined in his. His hands in her hair, his lips gently scraping her forehead. "*Miei sole, ed miei luna . . . miei amore.*" His breath was warm on her skin but the warmth that engulfed her came from within.

"What was that?" sleepily she asked him.

"My sun, my moon . . . my love." He'd said it. He loved her. He had loved her since he'd met her but had yet to admit it. Now he had. He wondered what she thought about it. Shifting so that he could see her face, he smiled glumly as he noted she had fallen asleep. She probably hadn't even heard him, he thought as he drifted into slumber himself.

After that day Macy had felt an escalation in their feelings and she thought that Jordan had felt it too. But lately she had begun to feel that Jordan was perfectly comfortable with their present arrangement. Every time they were together she hoped to hear him profess his love for her. But he never did. She was beginning to think that he would never have any substantial feelings for her.

Of course he cared about her, he showed that daily. Before he left the cottage he wanted to know what she was going to be doing, whom she would be with and where she would be. She knew that he was generally concerned about her and that he would do whatever she asked, but that didn't mean that he loved her, and she needed that. She was beyond the physical; she needed a deeper commitment. The problem was, what if Jordan didn't want that at all? What if all he wanted was a mistress?

She followed the path to a beautiful spot near the water. She sat under a tree and stared out at the sea. It was a perfect place to sit and think. And she needed to do just that. She planned to talk to Jordan tonight so she wanted all of her thoughts in order.

She pulled a seed from the pomegranate she brought and in the next instant frowned at its taste. Jordan had first introduced her to the fruit one night after they'd shared a long hot bath. He'd peeled it and carefully placed one sweet seed in her mouth at a time. Somehow the taste wasn't as sweet today as it was that night Macy thought sadly as she walked across a stretch of land near the water. There was a small hill with two trees at the top.

If Jordan didn't love her she would find the strength to walk away. She would return to L.A., move into her apartment and be his attorney only. She wondered now if he even needed her to work for him. Maybe he'd just wanted her as his lover. After all, he did say that he wanted her the first moment he saw her. He couldn't have known she was an attorney then.

But if he did want her she vowed to do everything in her power to keep him. She'd decided she would stay in L.A. and work, keeping her caseload light so she'd be able to spend time with Jordan.

Macy wanted this relationship to be different from the one she'd had with Steven. Admitting that she was getting ahead of herself, she slumped back against the tree.

"Oh, Jordan. What do we do now?" she asked herself. She lay her head back on the trunk of the tree as the breeze ruffled her hair.

"Too beautiful to be alone." The man's voice startled her. She dropped her fruit as she rose to meet him eye to eye.

"I'm sorry, do I know you?" He looked so familiar. His eyes were a deep brown and his shoulder-length hair was as black as the night. He was very attractive; she had to give him that.

"No. But I know you quite well," he said. She began to feel just

a little bit uncomfortable; he was looking at her a little too famil-
iarly. He looked familiar but his accent indicated he was not
American. His skin was darker than that of the Sicilians so Macy
surmised that he had to be mixed with something else. He almost
looked black.

"Are you staying at Pizzolungo?" Macy asked.

"Yes and no." The smile that covered his face clicked and she
recognized him instantly. "Mr. Masseretti?" she whispered.

"You remembered me. I'm flattered." He'd moved closer.

"Why are you here?" *There you go again, Macy, asking ques -
tions you really don't want to know the answers to.* This guy was
creepy, and she didn't like the way he looked at her.

His eyes were cold and he smiled menacingly at her.

"I'm wondering why you're all alone out here. If I were your
boyfriend I'd never let you out of my sight."

"You know what? I think I left my book back in the cottage. I
need to go and get it. If you'll excuse me," Macy said as she tried
to step past him.

"Oh no, little Macy. You won't be needing your book where
you're going. I'll entertain you personally," He smiled again, this
time chilling her blood.

He was quick and thorough. The needle had gone into her skin
effortlessly and Macy fell quietly into his arms. He looked down
into her face as he carried her to the boat he had anchored just south
of the hills. When he had reached the boat he lay her down gently
and lightly caressed her cheek. So soft he thought. She smelled just
like the sheets in the cottage. He watched her breasts rise and fall.
He wanted to take her right then, right there. But he refrained. He
would have to wait until he was home to enjoy her.

CHAPTER NINE

Three weeks after their arrival in Sicily, Jordan finally discovered that his father and his wife would be home the following day. Tony's cousin Tiago was able to sweet-talk one of the maids in Dioncello's household for this information. He also found out that his father had been planning a trip to the States until his mother-in-law had gotten sick. Why had he been planning a trip to the states? Matthew's anticipated funeral perhaps? Or maybe, a meeting with the Mafia?

Paris informed Jordan that though his grandfather had probably been involved with the Mafia, it was highly unlikely that his father was anything more than a wine merchant. Jordan couldn't get two things to match, but he felt in his bones that his father was involved in the deaths of his mother and Matthew.

He had decided that he would confront his father the next day, and if nothing came of their discussions, then he would leave the country. He would take Macy home and they would get on with their lives. Then the thought occurred to him that he didn't know if Macy wanted to continue as they were.

As far as he was concerned, he knew that she enjoyed his body as much as he enjoyed hers. The last few weeks of their relationship had been absolutely blissful, the perfect honeymoon. But as for Macy, he wasn't sure how she felt about him or their relationship. He presumed that she was not the type to take lovemaking lightly. That alone meant that she had to harbor some kind of emotion for him. But how deep were here feelings?

He would have to ask her, he decided. Rosalita had told him how Macy liked to take walks during the day. He would offer to take a walk with her. Maybe then she would relax enough to tell him how she felt about him.

When Jordan arrived at Pizzolungo, he knew instantly that something was not right. There was no one in the main courtyard. Someone was always out and about. Rosalita hadn't come out to greet him either. That was strange. She always made a point of greeting Jordan when he came in so that she could tell him about Macy's day. Now there was only quiet. A stab of alarm knifed through his stomach. Macy. Hurriedly he crossed the courtyard heading straight for the cottage. Mariella, the maid, came out of the big house and intercepted him.

"*Senor*, she not be there," she said sadly.

"What?"

"She gone. Rosalita go to see her this morning and she be gone. She walk and walk and not find her."

"Where is Rosalita?" Jordan demanded.

"She is resting. She was very upset about *senorita*. She say you be very upset with her. I tell her to lie down and I tell you the news."

"I don't understand. Where could she have gone?" She wouldn't leave him; he knew that in his heart. No, something else must have happened.

"*Senor* Jordan I am so sorry. I not watch her. I so sorry."

Jordan saw Rosalita emerging from the house. Her face was streaked with tears.

"It's okay, Rosalita. Just tell me what happened." He tried to remain calm.

"I go to see her like I always do after I see you go. She was not th re. I know she like to walk so I walk along the trail we go sometimes. I did not see her. I wait all day. She not come back. I check the cottage, her clothes still there, her comb and brush still there, but *senorita* not." Rosalita was crying again. Great big heart-wrenching sobs.

"Calm down, Rosalita. Is there anywhere else she would go? Someplace else she liked?"

"We find a hill with trees yesterday. She say 'so pretty, so quiet.' She like it very much." Ringing her hands the woman continued to cry.

"Good, Rosalita. Where is that hill?" Jordan mentally prayed that she had fallen asleep there. They had been up a good portion of the night, so she might have just been tired and lost track of the time.

He walked the path and followed the directions Rosalita had given him. She wasn't there but she had been, Jordan was sure. He found the half-eaten fruit and her almost empty water bottle. She would not have left this here on purpose. What could have happened? As he asked himself that question he felt the queasiness of real fear come over him. He sat on the hill and buried his face in his hands.

He had gotten her into this. He had endangered her life and now she was missing. Someone had taken Macy. His Macy. He had to get her back. He didn't care at this moment who had done what. He just wanted Macy back. She didn't deserve this. Hadn't he whispered that he would take care of her after they had made love? He had failed her. Now she would surely never love him the way he loved her.

His brain went into full gear. Her disappearance had to be connected to him and his investigation in some way, but how? Obviously this person had been following them or he would not have known about Macy. Jordan had been very careful to leave some things at a hotel a few blocks away from his father's estate to make it seem that he was staying there. He had even made a point of stopping at the hotel every day so that the employees there saw him. So whoever was doing this had been to Pizzolungo. Maybe he was a resident here. He suddenly remembered that she'd met a couple from Switzerland, but she hadn't understood them very well. He would find out who this couple was and then he would contact Tiago.

Next, he'd call Paris. Paris was his closest friend and the one person he could trust. He would call him tonight and tell him to get to Pizzolungo with all possible speed. He sincerely hoped that he would have Macy back before Paris arrived, but things didn't look good. Macy must be scared to death, not knowing what was going on. But she is smart. She would figure out what she needed to do to stay alive until he could get to her. At least he hoped she would.

Macy awoke slowly, afraid to open her eyes. She could feel the swaying of the water beneath her. She didn't know how she had come to be in this boat but she could tell that it wasn't a good trip she was taking. When she ventured to open her eyes, she saw the back of the man who was rowing. His dark hair hung loosely around his shoulders, and the muscles in his back were contracting as he worked the oars. Who was he? Closing her eyes again, she saw his face clearly, saw the smile and felt shivers go up her spine. He'd known her name. She hadn't told him that when they'd met that first day at Pizzolungo. *Well, apparently he'd been watching you, silly.* Why hadn't she seen him approaching? Probably because she was so deep in thought about Jordan. Jordan.

Would he think that she had left him? Probably not, Jordan was too confident of his effect on women to even entertain that thought. He would know that something had happened, and he'd count on her to help him find her if she could. She needed to figure out what was going on and why this man was taking her to God knows where. She shifted a bit so that she could look around and she saw a small cottage just off the shoreline; she figured that must be their destination. From a distance it didn't look like such a bad place. It wasn't a dungeon or anything like that.

What would happen once they got there, she thought. Refusing to give in to the panic that threatened, she closed her eyes, taking deep breaths in an effort to slow the rapid beating of her heart.

Her captor pulled the boat to shore and lifted her across his shoulder. She concentrated on being still so that he would think she was still unconscious. She needed to postpone their inevitable confrontation as long as possible. She heard him put a key into the lock, then push the door open. Stifling heat almost smothered her the moment they entered. In a moment he laid her down on a bed fragrant with rose oil, like Rosalita had given her.

As she heard him shuffling around the cottage she decided not to chance opening her eyes too soon. His movements stopped. She held her breath. Then he began to move toward her, she could tell because his footsteps sounded closer and closer. Her mind scrambled to think of something to do. She had to do something, she couldn't just let him take advantage of her or kill her or whatever it was he intended to do.

Cold water splattered against her face. She had trouble pretending that she hadn't felt that. Sputtering, she tried to focus clearly on the man who held her captive. He was tall and almost as big as Jordan. He wore jeans and a faded green sweatshirt. He certainly didn't look like a kidnapper. What did kidnappers look like these days? As if she had some idea.

"You are okay. Now you must wake up and talk to me," He sat on the bed next to her. Macy moved as close to the other end as she could without falling onto the floor.

"Now, now Macy. Don't be that way. There is no need for you to be afraid. I will not harm a hair on that pretty little head of yours. I just want to talk." He sounded almost sincere. But, Macy was still leery of him. She figured there was no use refusing to talk to him. Maybe it would help her figure out a way to get out of this place

"Why am I here?" she asked.

"Because you, like all the other fluffy-head American girls choose Jordan. That was a big mistake on your part." So it was about Jordan. Maybe he had found something in his investigation. No. He would have told her.

"I still don't understand. Who are you?" Sitting upright in the bed she could see him better. He didn't look as menacing as he had when he'd approached her earlier. Even though her hands were still bound she felt less intimidated when they were eye to eye.

"I guess you can not blame Jordan for what his parents did wrong," Reaching out he stroked her hair. Instinctively she flinched and moved away.

"I said I would not hurt you Macy. You need not worry." He was getting a little agitated now; she acted like he had a deadly disease or something. He was just as good as Jordan and he would show her that very soon.

"Well, then what is the point of this whole kidnapping thing? I truly don't understand what is going on, and I would appreciate it if you would just tell me the whole story instead of beating around the bush. That would be the only polite thing you've done today, you know." Macy was upset now. If it were true that he wouldn't hurt her she might as well speak her mind. And if it wasn't, she sure as hell was going to find out pretty soon if she continued to talk to him this way. Cold, dark eyes bore into her skin. She briefly wondered if he would change his mind and smack her for getting smart with him.

His eyes never wavered. It wasn't really a frightening stare; just a curious one. Kind of like the one Jordan always gave her when she argued with him. Like he was stunned that she even dared talk back to him.

"What is it that you want to know, little one?" He asked smiling.

"Who are you?" Macy thought that was the best place to start.

"I am Vincent Diago Penelli," He said and waited for her response. It hit her like a ton of bricks. He was Jordan's brother. But that's impossible; he hadn't said his name was Matthew. Jordan's brother's name was Matthew. She was confused.

"And you are?" She said looking puzzled.

"I am Jordan's brother." Seeing her confusion he continued, "His younger brother."

"Well. That explains the resemblance. Now why am I here?" As long as he was answering questions.

"You, my dear, are two things; one, an interesting diversion, and two, Jordan's Achilles' heal." He was apparently not going to tell her anymore than what she requested. She was happy to oblige, because as always she was full of questions.

"And that means what? I mean, I don't need you to tell me what an Achilles'heal is. I just don't understand my involvement or why you would kidnap someone for knowing your brother."

"Well, that's for another time. Now I want to talk about you, Macy. How did you come to meet Jordan?" She really did not want to go into this with him but he had been so good about answering her questions that she figured cooperation was her best defense.

She recapped the story of their first meeting leaving out the minor details of their physical attraction. She specifically mentioned the part about finding out about Matthew. She wanted to see Vincent's reaction to that. It was unsatisfying. He had absolutely no reaction, almost like she hadn't told him his brother had been killed. He listened patiently, watching her every move. Not that she thought he would do anything to her, but the way he was watching her was a little disconcerting.

"So, my brother wanted you and he took you. Now, I have done the same. What a coincidence." Laughing, Vincent moved closer to her on the bed.

"Well, why would you want me? You don't even know me!" Macy raised her voice.

"And neither did Jordan but you didn't seem to question him, now did you?" They were arguing like two children. Voices raised and tempers flaring. It would have been a comical scene had Macy not still been in a strange cottage, in a strange country, with a man she was quickly believing to be a lunatic.

"I didn't question him because it was not my job to do so. This on the other hand is borderline insane. You do not just take what you want when it concerns human beings. Did your parents ever teach you about stealing?" Angry beyond words now, Macy clenched the sheets below her. This Vincent person was really ticking her off. He reminded her so much of Jordan that it was causing a dull ache in her chest. She wanted to go back to Pizzolungo. She wanted Jordan to hold her again. She didn't want to be here with this man in this room. This was not in the plan.

Hadn't Steven warned her about this? The danger of this man and his family. Yeah, but on the other hand Steven hadn't treated her much better. After a year of dating he goes on a business trip to Nevada for a week and comes back married to some little chit that worked in one of the casinos.

Then, he'd betrayed her by siding with the partners about her moving to L.A. with a total stranger, only to call her days later warning her of impending danger.

A flurry of emotions swirled within her. She was pissed with Steven, not only for sending her to L.A. but for thinking that he could call her and warn her not to get involved with another man.

Then she was pissed with Jordan for getting her involved in his personal little mafia war, and leaving her alone to be kidnapped by his lunatic brother that he didn't even know existed.

And she was deathly afraid that she wouldn't see either man again to give him a piece of her mind.

The sound of Vincent's voice brought her back to her present situation.

"Yes they did as a matter of fact. Anything makes sense as long as you don't get caught." As he said these words a dark look came over him. He changed instantly. He lifted her from the bed and thrust her against the wall. Her head hit the paneling with a loud thump.

"Let's get this understood right now, Macy Glenn. You are here by my wish, which means that whatever I wish you to do, you will do and whatever I wish to do to you, you will oblige. Do you understand me?" She looked at him wordlessly. "I said, do you understand . . . ?" His face was so close to hers she could feel spittle slapping against her cheeks as he yelled at her.

"I heard you, you don't have to repeat yourself. Now put me down. This is not very hospitable of you," she said barely holding onto her temper, anger overriding fear. How dare he touch her in such a way. There was definitely a control problem with the Penelli men. He seemed to believe that since he had kidnapped her he could do what he wanted to her and that included being rude. Well he didn't know Macy Glenn at all. She would not bend to his will. He released her only so that her feet were now touching the floor, but he still held her imprisoned against the wall.

When he released her, quick as lightening Macy shot her knee into his groin and with a scream of pain he bent over, clutching his crotch. Macy watched him as he rolled across the floor. "That'll teach you to put your filthy hands on me again," She quickly scanned the room only to realize that running away was impossible. Through the window she could see water. Another window on the opposite side of the wall displayed a large body of water as well. She had no idea where she was or how the hell she would get back to Pizzolungo. Should she leave the cottage and get lost out there only to have Vincent come find her again and be pissed off that she had run away, changing his sociable mood to maniacal and deciding it would be better just to kill her, or wait here for Jordan who she hoped with all that was in her would come to her rescue?

Looking down at him she stared at the pitiful creature that he was. Macy thought she saw tears in his eyes. She had kicked him hard.

"I'm going to the bathroom." She stared at Vincent on the floor whining like a baby. "Would you like to join me? To ensure that I won't run away?" She said smiling prettily. Vincent was still trying to get his bearings. He saw her looming above him but she was a blurry haze. He could hear her voice, but he had no idea what she was saying.

"I guess not." Macy hunched her shoulders and walked away.

She walked into the kitchen and quickly realized that it wasn't the bathroom. There was only one other room besides the one Vincent lay in so she assumed that had to be it. Before going in she noticed that Vincent had made it to a sitting position, albeit still on the floor. He had stopped yelling and was now holding his bruised groin. "And if it's not too much trouble could you find me some-thing to eat? Because of you I've missed lunch," she said and closed the bathroom door behind her.

Once the large oak door had been securely closed behind her she let out the breath that she'd been holding. So he had meant what he said about not hurting her. She had done her damnedest to upset him enough to do her some harm, if he was capable of it, and he hadn't. Now she needed to figure out her next move. Since running away had already been ruled out, her only option was to befriend Vincent.

That would be a drastic change from the scene that just took place, but it was her only choice. As much as she wanted to find out why he had it in for Jordan, she would rather not spend any more time than necessary with Vincent. He was definitely unstable, and Macy didn't want to stick around long enough to find out how unstable. She shook her head at the image staring back at her in the mirror, realizing that she had no choice in the matter.

There was no mistake that Vincent was in charge, at least for now anyway. She quickly flushed the toilet, remembering that she was supposed to be using the bathroom. The last thing she needed was for him to get suspicious and come barging through the door. She fought back the urge to cry. She was trapped. For the second time in her life she felt as if all choices had been taken away from her. And who was at the other end of her dismay, Jordan Blake. Only she could fall in love with the man who in the last month had managed to turn her normal and decent life into shambles. Not only was she miles away from home, well actually oceans away from home, but she was now in the company of a madman.

She felt her resolve beginning to crumble. *Macy Glenn you will not do this!* You will not let him turn you into a blubbering idiot. He's not worth it and neither is his brother, no matter how much you love him. If she had to be a prisoner then she'd flip the script and be the best damned prisoner Vincent had ever seen.

She placed her hand on the doorknob and thought of Jordan. How would he know where to find her? Since he had failed to mention another brother, he probably didn't even know about Vincent. Which meant he probably wouldn't know where to look for her. He might not love her, but he wouldn't just abandon her. Or at least she hoped he wouldn't.

CHAPTER TEN

Three days had passed since Macy's disappearance and in that time Jordan had found nothing to help him locate her. There were no clues in the cottage. No phone calls. Nothing. Paris had arrived the evening after Macy's disappearance and became Jordan's right hand. He'd asked around the village immediately outside of Pizzolungo and had Tiago asking around in the city. Though he was confident that they would find her, he was going out of his mind with worry.

Jordan had paced the floors of the cottage until he could almost see a pattern of his footsteps. He thought of nothing but Macy. He couldn't sleep, he barely ate, he was totally lost without her. How could she have come to mean so much to him in such a short time? If he ever found her, he pledged never to let her out of his sight again.

Paris walked in on Rosalita's lecture to Jordan about keeping up his strength.

"You not be able to help *senorita* if you fall over from hunger," she was saying.

"She's right you know," Paris joined in. "Whoever has Macy may very well be the person who killed Matthew. How do you intend to fight him if you're dehydrated and malnourished?" Jordan knew they were right, but he had no appetite.

He continued to sit in the window seat staring out into the courtyard, a spot he had favored in the last few days. He felt close to Macy when he sat there. She had liked to sit there in the mornings as she watched him do his daily exercises. He remembered how pretty she looked with her knees drawn up to her chin and the streaks of copper in her hair shimmering in the sunlight.

"Have you found anything?" he asked without turning to face Paris. He heard Rosalita beginning to mumble again as she left the room.

"No. But Dioncello returned on Tuesday as scheduled. I think now would be a good time to go see him."

"I don't think so," was all Jordan could say.

"Jordan, do you love this woman?" Paris asked. He was all but certain that his friend had finally fallen in love.

"What difference does it make? It's my fault she's in this mess. She's my responsibility whether I love her or not."

"It makes a world of difference. Yes, she is your responsibility, and it is your fault she's been taken, but have you tried to think of why she was taken in the first place?" Paris sat down in a chair a few steps away from Jordan.

"What do you mean?"

"I can see what this woman has come to mean to you by the way you've been looking the past couple of days. Now, just think a minute. The person who kidnapped her must know that too. He must have been watching you since Matthew's death or how would he have known to find you here?" Jordan could see where Paris's mind was going and he began to think along with him.

"So, if he followed me here, then he would know where Macy was staying despite my trying to keep her hidden."

"If he followed you here, he's probably still here." Paris said.

"I've already checked with Mariella. The only people who came when we did were the couple from Switzerland, the Masserettis."

"Did you talk to them?" Paris asked.

"No, they checked out last week,"

"Maybe they did, but what if that was part of the plan?" Paris knew that he had struck a cord with Jordan; he could see his mind clicking.

"But why Macy? It would make more sense for me to be the target." Jordan began to pace the floor again.

"What better way to get to you than to take the love of your life?" Paris studied him. "That is what she is, isn't she?"

Paris and Jordan had been friends since middle school. When they first met Jordan had been shy and leery of making friends. Paris, always boisterous and outgoing, had befriended him. When they got into their first fistfight together over a cute little honey in algebra class, who coincidentally rejected both of them, their friendship had been sealed for life. No one knew him as well as Paris. Next to Matthew, he'd been all the family Jordan had ever needed.

"I thought I would never love anyone this completely. I actually never wanted to until I saw her. I just knew Paris, I just knew. We've been so happy these past couple of weeks. Things were going so well. I was going to tell her that I was ready to give up the investigation so that we could go home and live a normal life. But then she was gone. She doesn't even know that I love her," Jordan said quietly.

"Jordan, if I could see how much you care for her without seeing you with her, you can just imagine what this maniac saw when you two were together. I think that whoever this person is, he has a vendetta against you. If it were someone who worked for your father or someone who wanted to get at your father, taking Macy wouldn't make any sense at all. But if he wanted to get at you, then she would be the perfect pawn." Paris rose to stand beside Jordan.

He gently touched his shoulder.

"We are dealing with a very dangerous person here. I think we should talk to your father or contact the police."

"No! I won't go running to him with my problems!" Jordan yelled. After some consideration he said, "But I will visit him, just in case he is connected somehow. As for the police, not yet. When I find this person, and I will find him, I want him all to myself. I don't need the police trying to intervene. Now I'm going to Santiaga to see my father." Jordan stood and walked out of the room.

Paris sat on the bed mulling over what they had just discussed. He knew that Dioncello was still connected to Macy's disappearance as well as Matthew's murder. Jordan's concern for Macy would make him too emotional to get the answers they needed, so he would have to do most of the legwork on his own. He didn't mind, of course. Jordan had been very good to him, giving him a job even though he had barely made it through law school and had passed the bar only after four tries at it, not to mention taking care of him when he had that bout with drugs a few years earlier.

Paris remembered when he had been in an old abandoned house on the streets of San Francisco blasted out of his mind and Jordan had saved him. He had been there for him. He had given him the strength to go on and now he would return the favor as best he knew how. He owed him this much; he would find his woman for him.

The iron gates to Villa Santiaga opened slowly as Jordan walked through them for only the second time in his life. On the ride over he had had lots of time to consider what he would say to his father, how he would inquire into his personal life without his suspecting anything. As he waited for someone to answer the door, he remembered Macy's observations about him and his father. She had wanted him to be more open-minded about what had happened years ago. He would love to be able to do that, if not for himself, for her. But he honestly didn't see how he could. Especially if it turned out that his father was somehow connected to her disappearance.

Maria came to the door as he had expected. She wasn't quite sure what to say, so he said it for her.

"I know he's here, Maria. You can announce me or I'll announce myself. It's your call," he said solemnly.

"Come in," she said. She closed the door behind him and walked through the large hall. When she returned a short while later, he knew that she had not only alerted his father of his presence but his wife as well. Tiago had informed him that Maria had come along with Mrs. Penelli when she married, so her loyalty would forever lie with her. He was ushered into a dark room filled with deep mahogany furniture and dismal tapestries. The walls gave off a very cold and angry aura. A man sat staring out the window, his broad frame seeming to rest sullenly in the chair.

"You have finally felt the need to see me?" he said without turning to look at Jordan.

"I have some questions that needed to be answered and you're the only one who can answer them," Jordan replied. He had to admit that just being in his father's presence was intimidating. Butterflies moved through his stomach at an astronomical pace. But he stood his ground and held himself proudly.

"So ask your questions." Despite what he'd told Macy, Jordan had hoped he would be received more cordially by his father. But why should he have hoped that? It had always been apparent that his father wanted nothing to do with him.

"Did you kill my mother and Matthew?" His anger made him blunt.

"Is that what you think? Do you think that your own father would be capable of such a thing?"

"I don't know what to think and I would like to stop assuming what happened. If you know something, I am asking that you tell me now."

Dioncello stood and turned to face his eldest son. Their resemblance was astonishing. Only Dioncello's graying hair and his protruding belly and Jordan's obvious darker complexion set them apart.

"You are as your mother envisioned you would be. I have followed your success in America. "Theresa would have been proud." Jordan winced at the sound of his mother's name coming from this man.

"I do not wish to waste your time. I just want answers,"

"I never meant to intentionally hurt Theresa, but in the end I guess that's what I did by leaving. And I would never harm a child of mine." He stared at Jordan intently.

Jordan believed him because he had looked him in the eye and told him. Despite how much Jordan wanted to deny it, Dioncello seemed sincere. When he spoke his mother's name he had even looked a little hurt. But that couldn't be.

"A friend of mine has disappeared. Do you know anything about it?"

"You mean your girlfriend? An attractive American girl?" Dioncello crossed the room to sit on the sofa. "She reminds me much of Theresa when we first met, so young, so beautiful, so strong." Dioncello was momentarily taken back thirty years. "It

takes a strong woman to leave everything she knows behind to follow a man for love. I see that Macy has adjusted well." Eyeing his
son closely, he watched as complete understanding of what he had
just said sank in.

Tense, his expression blank, Jordan asked, "How do you know
about her?"

"Jordan, you are my son. I know everything about you and
your life. Despite what you may think, I have been very involved in
your life."

"Then you know who has her?"

"No, I don't. But I wish I did. You know, Jordan, I didn't really want your mother to take you away but I was forced to allow it.
I have regretted that day ever since. I loved your mother and you
boys dearly," he waited, watching for Jordan's reaction.

"But you let us go anyway." Jordan couldn't help it. He had
planned not to discuss the past, but a part of him desperately wanted to know why his father had done what he had.

"Salvatore Marcionne, the father of the girl I had been
betrothed to, was a force to be reckoned with. My parents didn't
want to have to fight that battle. It was much easier to demand that
their only son do their bidding. I had married your mother in secre-
cy, because I knew that they would not approve. She wasn't
Sicilian. She wasn't even Italian; she was a black American. That
was more than unacceptable in my father's eyes. I do not blame my
parents for doing what they thought was best for me. I blame myself
for being so foolish and so cowardly that I did not stand up to them.
It cost me the love of my life and my children. That, Jordan, is a
burden I will carry with me to my grave." The man who stood
across the room from him was not the man Jordan had envisioned.
This man looked genuinely regretful.

"I see. I can't say that I feel much sympathy for you, but at least now I know a little more than I did before. I'm sorry if my coming here has opened up old wounds for you. I will see my way out." Jordan turned to leave the room.

"Jordan, you should know that you have another brother." That sentence stopped Jordan in his tracks. Another brother? Since when did he have a brother other than Matthew?

Jordan turned around in surprise. "What are you talking about?"

"When your mother left with you boys, she was pregnant. She contacted me about two months after she arrived in the States. Santina could not have children of her own and the Penelli name needed to go on. My father suggested that Theresa have the baby and send it to Sicily to live with us as Santina's child. Theresa reluctantly agreed, realizing that it would be even harder to take care of three children on her own. So, the child was raised as the only Penelli heir until my father's death." Dioncello lit a cigar. He seemed weary.

"You took my mother's baby? It wasn't enough for you to disgrace her, cheat on her and then abandon her, and your two children? You had to take more from her? Why? Oh, because your father told you to. Tell me something, Dad," Jordan said sarcastically, "if he had asked you to take a knife to my mother and us would you have done that too?" His fingers shook with the ferocity of his anger.

"I would never have caused you any harm. Any of you. I loved you all. I wanted us to be together, but that couldn't be." Jordan was astounded. That this man could stand here and tell him this was unbelievable.

"You knew it couldn't be when you met her. Why didn't you leave her alone? She could have married one of her own people and been happy. She wouldn't have had to live in poverty caring for two children on her own. You, Father, are a poor excuse for a man." Jordan had heard enough. The rage that had been pent up inside of him for the last twenty-five years was about to erupt. He needed to leave this place, before he did something they would both regret.

"Vincent has always been very jealous of you, Jordan." Jordan continued to walk into the hallway. Dioncello followed him and stood in the doorway.

"He might be involved in Macy's kidnapping." That gave Jordan pause. His feelings for his father had nothing to do with this visit. His priority was Macy. He'd deal with the rest later.

"Why would he want her?" Jordan knew the answer as he spoke the question. And guilt for his role in Macy's disappearance began to overtake him.

"Come back in and sit down, I do not wish for anyone to hear us." Dioncello motioned to Jordan and waited while his son wrestled with the decision to go or stay.

When Jordan came back in the room, Dioncello carefully closed the door and took his seat at his desk. "It's probably not so much wanting her, as it is wanting to hurt you."

"Did he kill my mother and Matthew?" He had to know. He needed to know what he was dealing with.

"Jordan, you must understand. Vincent grew up an outsider in this house. Santina never really got over the fact that he was Theresa's child. One day in a drunken rage she told Vincent of his true heritage. He left and I did not see him for well over a year. When he returned, he seemed bitter and hateful. We had never been especially close, but now we are worlds apart. I cannot say if he killed anyone; I can only tell you that he is very angry. Because you seem to have a successful life in America, he thinks that somehow he was cheated."

"I don't understand." Leaning forward resting his arms on his

103

knees he waited for the answers to come.

"You are my first born, and naturally, my heir. Only I couldn't claim you as such all those years. So after my father's death I had my will changed. I wanted you to have what was rightfully yours." Watching the blank expression on Jordan's face, Dioncello clarified the situation for him. "Everything I have, everything I am would fall on your shoulders upon my death."

"I don't need anything you have and I don't want to be what you are." His jaw clenching, Jordan continued to stare at the man who had changed his life.

"I have loved you with all my heart since the day you were born. When your mother took you away she took a part of me with her. When Vincent was born I tried . . . I tried like hell to love him like a father should love his son, and in all technicalities his heir, as well." Rubbing his temples as if to ward off the pain Dioncello sat back in his chair. He'd come this far. There was no reason to stop now. "He is my child, my flesh and blood and I love him, but I had already lost so much. I tried! I really did! I tried to shower him with attention and love, but as he grew older it became harder. I was keeping tabs on you and Matthew, and I wanted my family. I wanted all of us together. I guess my despair was conceived as lack of interest to Vincent."

With his hands steepled at his chin he slowly shook his head, "I don't know. I've made so many mistakes. I've ruined so many lives." Old pain renewed wrenched through Dioncello's body.

"And as your heir, I inherit upon your death. Not Matthew and not Vincent." Jordan rolled his eyes. "So this is all about money. Your money. Shit!" Jordan paced the room.

"Matthew and Vincent would still receive a good amount of money upon my death, but the estate, the business, the legacy, it all comes to you. I don't know if that's all its about, but I'm sure it plays a big part. I don't know who killed Theresa or Matthew. I wish I did. I'd rest a lot easier at night if I knew."

"You aren't helping me!" Jordan yelled.

"I am so sorry Jordan. I truly do not know. I have told you all I know."

"Where can I find your son?" Cold distance colored Jordan's voice as he referred to his brother as Dioncello's son.

"He has a cabin on the coast of Milazzo." Dioncello watched the emotions flickering across Jordan's face. "You will go there, won't you?"

"Yes, I'm going there, and if this Vincent has hurt one hair on her head I will kill him. I will kill your son. So if you want to warn him, you do that, but I will find him and he will pay for what he has done," Jordan turned and walked out of the house. He never looked back.

That night Macy lay in the bed with the fresh sheets she had put on them this morning. Vincent was at his usual post sitting in a chair behind the door so that he could see if someone tried to come in at night and yet still watch Macy as she slept. She had discovered that he liked watching her, as if he was memorizing every move she made.

Macy didn't know why but she felt a strange kind of compassion for Vincent. Yeah, that was weird, feeling compassion for the person who held you captive. But he wasn't mean to her and now she knew he wouldn't hurt her. Her initial fear on the hill had been dissipated once they'd gotten to the cottage.

Vincent seemed so vulnerable to her. She didn't know the full story of his life, but if it were anything compared to Jordan's, then he deserved a bit of compassion from her. She still wanted to get the hell out of that cabin, but a part of her wanted to help Vincent with whatever it was that had forced him to do this.

In accordance with her plan to befriend him, she cooked and cleaned for him. He allowed her freedom to roam as long as she stayed in the cabin. When he had to leave he would lock the door from the outside and put a thick piece of wood against it so she couldn't get out. The windows, she discovered, were nailed shut. Already having decided that escape was hopeless, she waited less than patiently for Jordan.

Vincent had assured her that he would come to her rescue. The problem was that her rescue would also be his demise. Macy tried not to think of it that way. Things would work out for her and Jordan. They just had to!

They walked along the beach in total silence, hand in hand. Coming to a hill with two trees atop it, they sat and held each other close. He cupped her chin and lifted her face to receive his kiss. His lips touched hers, warm and comforting. Then his tongue, thick and hot, made its way into her mouth. She begged for more. Long slow strokes had him moaning with pleasure. His hands cupped the back of her head and held her in exactly the right position. She enveloped him in her arms and opened herself to him.

The sun began to set behind the hill as he entered her. Jordan moved slowly atop her, coming almost completely out of her before plunging back into the moist oblivion. Macy held him close as she marveled in the pleasure of having him hot and hard inside her. Her heart beat frantically as she neared her surrender; her cove drenched him with her satisfaction. When Jordan exploded inside her, her world was complete.

Macy turned fitfully on the bed and dreamed of her one true love.

CHAPTER ELEVEN

Jordan had gotten much more than he had bargained for on this trip. He had started out with the best intentions: to find out who murdered his brother. Not only had he failed at doing that, but he had walked an innocent woman directly into his unknown brother's plan to seek revenge against him. He went back to the cottage to mull over all of this newfound information and figure out his next move.

After eating some pasta that Rosalita had left for him, he'd taken a long, hot shower. Now he sat in the window seat thinking of the woman he had to save. He would meet with Paris early tomorrow morning and they'd put a plan in place. The clock was ticking and Jordan knew that Macy's life depended on him and what steps he took.

As he stared out into the night, he thought of the short time he and Macy had had together. It just wasn't fair. Some men, his father came to mind, experienced the love of a great woman and let her walk out of their lives. But after he had chanced upon such a woman, and allowed himself to love her, she had been taken from him. By his brother, no less. Yes, he felt certain that Vincent had taken Macy. Crazy as it was, it made sense.

Jordan had to be smart. He had to locate Vincent and meet him head to head. Going in with guns blazing wouldn't help; in fact it would probably ensure Macy's death. No, if what Dioncello had told him was true, Vincent wanted him. And him alone. He wanted the confrontation and Jordan was eager to give it to him.

Jordan assumed that Vincent had felt his mother didn't want him much like Jordan had grown up feeling that his father hadn't wanted him. And given the way Jordan felt about his father, he could certainly understand Vincent's frustration and anger. What he didn't understand was why he had been made the bad guy in this. He had lived his life the best way he knew how, and because of that he was successful. He was not the one who was raised with the Penelli fortune to speak for him. No, in college he had worked at McDonald's to help pay his tuition.

The Penelli fortune had never been in his life. So what did Vincent resent him for? He couldn't figure it out but then it didn't really matter. He did resent him, and that resentment had placed Macy in grave jeopardy.

But none of that was important now. His priorities had changed. He wasn't so concerned with finding his family's murderer as he had been before. Macy had changed that. With her outspoken views and total honesty she had given Jordan what he thought he had lost when his family was killed. She had shown him how to love. He didn't want to lose that too. And he vowed this night that he wouldn't.

When Macy awoke she heard voices. Vincent was talking to another man right outside the door. She couldn't understand what they were saying exactly, but the man sounded upset.

"You had better not mess up the plan, Vinnie. I don't know what you needed her for anyway."

Macy heard him stomp off the porch; she slipped out of the bed and went to the window. He got into a black Jeep, which meant there had to be a road nearby. Not that it would help her any. She wasn't left alone long enough to make a run for the door; besides Vincent always bolted it shut anyway. She hurried into the bathroom before Vincent could see that she was awake.

Quickly taking a shower she slipped into the jeans Vincent had provided, along with underwear and other clothing. She had to admit, this was a well planned kidnapping. Vincent had provided her with a complete wardrobe. The fact that everything was exactly her size unnerved her. How had he known her size? And what exactly had he had in mind when he bought all these clothes?

When she came out of the bathroom, Vincent slipped up behind her and placed his hands on her shoulders. Icy shivers ran down her body.

"Good morning. How are you today?" he said in an alarmingly nice voice, which was in stark contrast to the way she had just heard him speaking.

"I'm uh . . . fine considering the circumstances. How about you?" She still wasn't comfortable with him touching her, but remembering her plan to befriend him, she tried to ignore it.

"I would be so much better if I could feel your body against mine. Is that possible, Macy?"

She was repulsed and alarmed. And she couldn't help her immediate reaction to his question.

"No, it certainly is not!" She whipped around to stare at him. He had a strange glassy look in his eyes. A look she hadn't seen until now. And he began running his hands roughly up and down her arms.

"Come on, Macy, don't pretend that you don't want me because I know you do." He pulled her to him and began to grind his pelvis against her. "You know you want it."

She remembered hearing another member of the Penelli family saying the same thing to her. The problem was it was true in his case. In this case, however, it was not. She had begun to feel nauseous at the idea of Vincent touching her in such an intimate way. Closing her eyes she braced her palms against his chest and attempted to push him away.

Obviously stoned from some type of drug, his breathing was erratic as Macy shoved him with all her might. He stumbled into the table but managed to grab her as she made a move for the door. Screaming in Italian, he threw her on the bed.

Tears stung Macy's eyes as she tried not to think of what would come next. She had foolishly thought that Vincent had no intention of hurting her, and now he was attacking her. She opened her mouth to scream but his mouth crushed down on her and she felt his hands on her breasts.

She pounded on his back but he seemed oblivious to her meager assault. He lifted his head and tore at her clothing like a ravenous animal.

"Vincent, please don't do this," she pleaded.

"What? Forget Jordan! I'm better than he is! Much better!" When he lifted her up and ripped her jeans down, she screamed with all the strength she had in her. He retaliated with a blow that knocked her unconscious.

"*Bella*? Can you hear me? Come on, wake up now. It's me, Jordan."

She heard his voice and she felt his touch, but she thought she must have been dreaming again. Jordan wasn't there. She was with

Vincent. She began to cry, great big sobs.

Jordan cradled her in his arms and made soft shushing noises. "It's all right, you're safe now, *Bella*. You're safe." He stroked her hair and rocked her gently. How could he ever have put her in this situation? None of this would have happened if he hadn't insisted that she come with him.

She'd been hurt. A faint bruise had formed along the side of her face where Vincent had struck her. Lightly Jordan's fingers caressed the spot, his heart breaking with the tears that streamed from her eyes.

He'd done this. His family had done this. How could he even begin to hope that she'd still want to be with him after this? Knowing Macy, as soon as she fully came around, she'd probably hit him, then give him a piece of her mind, then leave him for good. Panic seared through him. He couldn't let that happen. He couldn't lose her; the last week without her had been horrible. He couldn't imagine their separation being permanent.

"Macy darling, please. It's okay now," he repeated. "I'm here, you're safe. Everything's alright now."

She opened her eyes slowly. Her vision was blurred by the tears. She touched his face, his eyes, his lips. It *was* him. Jordan had come for her finally. Finally. She had been Vincent's captive for almost a week and he had just gotten here.

"What took you so long? I've been here all week. Some night in shining armor you are," Macy murmured and tried to sit upright.

Jordan just smiled. Macy could always argue. It didn't matter what it was, she could argue about it. And hadn't he just envisioned her doing this. He brushed away her tears and kissed her cheeks.

"I love you, *Bella*," he said and lightly kissed her lips.

Stopping short with the rest of her argument, Macy stared at him. "Oh, Jordan. Do you really? I mean, at first I thought you just wanted to go to bed with me, and then I thought you might have developed some feelings for me, but then you changed again. I've been so confused. I prayed that I would get the chance to tell you how I felt about you and. . ." she began to cry again.

"So now I'm here. You can tell me now, *Bella*." He pushed strands of hair from her face.

"You know, Jordan, since you've met me you've called me 'Bella.' I think it means something good but I'm not sure."

"It means 'beautiful,' Macy."

"Beautiful. You think I'm beautiful. Jordan, you are so sweet." She kissed him this time.

"I thought you were waiting for the chance to tell me how you feel about me," he managed to say between kisses.

"Oh, I almost forgot. I love you, Jordan Blake. Even though you moved me to L.A., then dragged me to Sicily where I was kidnapped by your psychopath brother and . . . oh God, Jordan he. . ." He saw the fear come into her eyes and knew instinctively what she was thinking.

"No, darling, he didn't get the chance to do anything to you. We got here just in time."

Jordan had left early that morning with Paris and Tiago. He had told them the story that Dioncello had cited to him. Paris had been following up on leads to the Masserettis. It seemed as though they had just vanished, thus giving Paris the impression that Vincent had been portraying Mr. Masseretti so that he could be closer to Jordan and Macy. But what had happened to Mrs. Masseretti? The thought that Vincent had done all these things alone still unsettled him. He and Jordan had agreed that there was more to this story, and that Dioncello knew a lot more than he was telling. They had decided to deal with him after Macy was safe.

As soon as they pulled up to the cottage he'd heard Macy

scream. His world had stopped. He'd kicked in the door and seen Vincent trying to pull her clothing off. Touching her, touching *his* Macy. He was on him in an instant, ready to kill him, pounding him mercilessly. Finally, Tiago had managed to pull him off.

Breathing hard, Jordan rushed to Macy and scooped her up into his arms, where she now rested.

"We?" Macy said realizing that they were not alone. She looked down and saw that someone, some blessed someone, had covered her.

"Macy I'm glad that you're safe. I don't know what we would have done with Jordan had some harm come to you." Paris smiled warmly at her. "And you remember Tiago, Tony's cousin."

"Macy smiled at Tiago as he stood staring at her blankly. Macy wasn't sure but she thought the young man was blushing.

On the floor, now tied and gagged, sat Vincent. Macy noted the bruises on his face and attributed them to Jordan whose right knuckles were also bruised. He wouldn't look at her. But Macy felt a sudden sadness staring at him, sitting there in his own little world. It was hard to imagine that Vincent and Jordan shared the same genes.

"Where's the other guy?" Macy asked suddenly.

"What other guy?" Jordan said.

Vincent lifted his head at the question. Though his cold black eyes glinted at Macy, the gag in his mouth kept him silent.

"There were two of them. I heard them talking this morning about Vincent not messing up the plan." Jordan had shared Macy enough for the time being. He wanted to get her back to the cottage as soon as possible.

"We'll discuss that after you've had a nice warm bath." Carrying Macy in his arms, Jordan began to walk towards the door.

"What do we do with him, Jordan?" Paris pointed to Vincent.

"We'll bring him back with us and call the authorities when we've finished talking to him." Jordan didn't spare Vincent another glance. He would never be a brother to him, not after what he had done to Macy, and quite possibly to his real brother.

In the boat, Macy fell asleep slumped against Jordan's massive chest. She seemed to be resting peacefully, and Jordan thanked God for keeping her safe. He said nothing when they brought Vincent aboard. He would deal with him later. For now his mind was reeling trying to figure out who the other man could have been. He would ask Macy for more details after she rested.

Much as he never wanted to see Dioncello again, he knew he had no choice. His father had known that Vincent had it in for Jordan, that Vincent was emotionally unstable, yet he had never bothered to tell him. Jordan had learned of the situation only because he had taken the initiative. And Dioncello had known quite a bit about Macy. In all likelihood, he had known positively that Vincent had taken her. Why had he given him only bits and pieces of information? What was he hiding and why was he hiding it?

Jordan reminded himself that though his father had seemed sincere in professing his love, he had cared only enough to keep tabs on them while they lived in the states but not enough to come for them. A lot of things didn't add up. In any event, he and Paris would figure it all out once they got back to the village. For sure he would keep Macy at his side constantly. He would not risk losing her again.

CHAPTER TWELVE

The next week was heaven for Macy and Jordan. They spent all of their time together, mostly in bed. On the evening of their return Jordan had not let her out of his sight. He had showered with her, washed her hair and even dried it with the blow dryer afterwards, a task he thoroughly enjoyed. Rosalita had come by to welcome her home, leaving bowls and bowls of food for them and muttering about Macy having lost weight in the week she had been away. They tasted a little bit of everything she had brought in.

"I've gained at least ten pounds tonight, I'm sure." Macy said as she removed their dishes from the table.

"It's good for you. We can't have you looking malnourished, now can we?" Jordan teased. "Why don't you leave the dishes there? I can get them later."

"It's okay, I can do it." Not wanting to argue so soon after her return he sat and watched her while she washed the dishes, marveling in the love he felt for her. He was content with his life for the first time. Because of Macy.

"All done. So what do you want to do now? I know. Let's take a walk. We could use it after the dinner we just had." She had moved to the closet door and was reaching for her sweater, as Jordan stopped her.

"No, we will not be going for a walk tonight, *Bella*." At the sound of his endearment, Macy felt shivers up her spine. She turned into the welcomed embrace of his arms, remembering how it felt to be apart and each silently hoping never to go through such a time again.

"I need you so much, *Bella*," Jordan whispered into her hair.

"Jordan, I was afraid. I thought I would never see you again." She had to get past the lump forming in her throat to say the words.

"Me, too, *Bella*, me too. I couldn't bear the thought of not seeing you again," He began to press feather-like kisses on her neck. Macy arched her back so that he could have complete access to her neck and felt a stirring in her midsection. Jordan lifted her into his arms and carried her into the bedroom, placing her on the bed ever so gently.

With his elbows supporting his weight he leaned over her and gently nipped her bottom lip before lightly kissing her.

Macy lifted her hand to caress his face. Holding him close she deepened the kiss. Jordan followed her lead while gently kneading her soft pliant bottom.

When he lowered himself to rest completely on top of her she could feel his arousal against her belly. She reached down into the sweat pants that he wore and encouraged his passion. His hardness filled her hands and pulsed with pleasure, as his kisses became more demanding.

Long dark fingers removed the clasp of her bra and lingered over the smooth mounds of her breasts. Taking a nipple between his fingers he brought it to a glorious peak. Macy's breath hitched at the tingling pleasure that ripped through her body. When he took the hardened pebble into his mouth, she sighed with delight.

Completing the assault on her breasts he moved slowly down to shower his attentions on the small indentation of her belly. His tongue flickered quickly in and out of the small crevice expertly.

Macy dug her nails into his shoulder anticipating the moment when he would end this sweet torture.

After removing her pants Jordan grabbed the rim of her panties with his teeth and proceeded to pull them down her legs. Macy thought she would explode at any moment.

Quickly he removed his clothes and returned to her on the bed. "Open for me." He said in a gruff voice. Macy kept her eyes on his as she widened her legs. There was no modesty, no shyness and no shame. This was her man. She trusted him with her life and she loved him with all her heart.

Jordan could see the glistening moistness and his mouth watered. Overcome by a desperate need to taste her, he lifted her legs to rest on his shoulders and followed his desire. The smell of her nectar rose through the air and teased him mercilessly. When his tongue made first contact Macy almost hopped off the bed.

"I know *Bella*, I feel it too." He said before trailing his tongue along the borders of her cove, stopping briefly at the small bud that sprung to life in response to his clever ministrations. He suckled, he licked, he loved her completely. And when Macy thought she could bear nothing more, when she felt limp from the roller coaster ride he had taken her on, he entered her.

Swiftly and ferociously his manhood delved into her. Deeper and deeper he carried her over the edge. With slow penetrating strokes he brought her to another release. A light sheen of sweat covered her body and she would have sworn that she had melted into the bed until he lifted her into the air and held her there.

With her legs wrapped tightly around his waist, he entered her again. Macy held on to him and swayed with the rhythm he had created.

Carrying her to the window seat, Jordan incessantly chanted into her ear. She had no idea what he said, of course, it was Italian, but it sounded beautiful just the same. She would never forget Sicily and she'd do everything in her power to keep this man.

Sitting in the window seat Jordan held her, waiting for her to ready herself for him again. He'd watched her fall into that oblivious sea of pleasure just moments before and didn't think she could take it again so soon, so instead he held her. Stroking her smooth skin he whispered, "You are my world, Macy. I cannot live without you."

"I won't leave you," she whispered to him. His eyes held hers and he prayed that what she said was true.

"You are all that I have."

"You are all that I want." With that said and her passion renewed, Macy positioned herself to receive him. She rode him swiftly and passionately with an energy that surprised even herself. Jordan dug his fingers into the soft skin of her bottom and held her still for his release. With his head thrown back, he roared with the force of the climax, "I love you." The words were strangled in his throat.

"And I love you." Macy said as she held his head against her chest. "I will always love you."

CHAPTER THIRTEEN

A week later Jordan had gained no more information. After trying to speak with Vincent and getting no answers, Jordan had decided against talking to his father again. Vincent would be jailed and the plot of revenge would be locked away with him.

Who had actually killed his mother and Matthew, and why, remained a mystery, but Jordan's priority had shifted. He wanted to get Macy home safely. Endangering her life for answers he might never get would end now. He booked them on a flight out of Sicily and left Paris behind to see if anybody showed up looking for Vincent.

The trip had proved to be successful in only one respect: he had fallen deeply in love. He and Macy would return to L.A., and he would get on with his life with her by his side. If Dioncello and Vincent were the true culprits behind the deaths of his mother and brother, then it would be up to the police to uncover the truth. A small part of him harbored the guilt of not seeking justice for Matthew's murder, but that part of him could not be satisfied.

He had something more important now. Something that needed to be nourished and appreciated. The danger of finding a killer had been unnerving, and he had no desire to tempt fate. Jordan would not further involve himself with Macy.

At the cottage in Malizzo an angry man paced the floor. He'd known that Vincent's obsession with that woman was going to affect the plan he had so carefully arranged. Now Vincent was in jail and Jordan was undoubtedly returning to the States very soon. What would he do now? He had to end this and soon. Time was running out. If only the girl were not in the picture. He had never intended to hurt anyone besides the people who stood in the way of his fortune.

Because Jordan looked so much like Dioncello, Theresa had always seemed to favor him over her younger son. Life had been good to Jordan. He'd enjoyed love from his mother, a college education and now a great career. He doubted that Jordan even knew about what else he had acquired through his heritage. But he did. He knew it all too well and he hated it. Surely he was meant to have something, something more than just a name that would get him nowhere.

He and Vincent were two of a kind and that was why they had made such a good team in the beginning. Both their childhoods had been unhappy. They hadn't seemed to be wanted by either of their parents. Vincent had been raised by a drunken woman who despised him and a father who could barely stand to be in the same room with him.

As adults, they both shared the same feelings of hatred for Theresa and Jordan and had come up with the perfect plan to exact their revenge. Unfortunately, Vincent had been attracted by that silly woman who was obviously in love with Jordan, and had jeopardized everything.

So what now, he wondered. Should he return to the States with them and end this once and for all or should he cut his losses and take the meager amount allotted to him upon Dioncello's death. He was easily shielded from accusation in either country, since they all believed him to be dead.

That had been the most ingenious part of his plan. In order to avoid fingers being pointed at him, he had faked his death with Vincent's help. A little money could buy anything. It had been simple enough to pay someone to replace his dental records with those of the man he'd killed and left at the bottom of the cliffs in Vegas. It had been even easier to make it look like a murder, so similar to the one that had been committed seven years before. Killing the unsuspecting motorist hadn't been pleasant but it was necessary.

His mother's death had been a little more difficult. His anger and hatred had not been enough for him to actually kill her himself, so he'd paid a hefty sum to have that done for him. But Vincent had gotten sloppy when he'd seen that girl. Now Jordan surely knew who Vincent was and was possibly piecing things together.

The plan had been simply to get Jordan out of the way so that he would become Dioncello's lawful heir. He would then inherit everything and he'd take care of Vincent. Then they'd simply wait for Dioncello to go, his heart wasn't good anymore and it was just a matter of time. But his mother had gotten in the way and so he'd had to remove her from the equation first. Now, Vincent had let Jordan slip through their hands because of his fascination with that woman. Macy was her name, he thought cynically. She'd messed things up royally. Now she'd have to pay as well.

The plane ride was quiet as Macy sat with her thoughts and Jordan with his. This had been a trying six weeks for both of them and it wasn't over. They both knew that once they were back in L.A. things would be different.

They would no longer be in Sicily. They both had jobs and commitments in the States. What would happen now that they had discovered their love for each other?

Macy remembered her vow to do whatever she could to keep Jordan. She believed that Jordan loved her and she knew she loved him but she still had reservations about what he really wanted from her. He'd never said he wanted to get married. He only said that he loved her and wanted her. Was that a commitment or simply an admission?

Jordan remembered Macy's ambition and strong objections to moving to L.A. He had wondered what she would do when they returned. Would she continue living in his house or would she prefer going to a hotel?

The time they'd spent together in the cottage had been unforgettable, but Macy was a determined woman. Jordan knew she had career aspirations that up until now had guided all her decisions in life. He desperately hoped some of that had changed.

When they reached L.A. the air was thick with humidity, and the sun blazed from its position in the sky. What had been so pretty from the airplane window was now a hot, humid concrete jungle. Or maybe it was just her mood. Macy couldn't decide.

Joseph was waiting for them at the car, and he smiled as he helped Macy into the backseat.

"Did you enjoy yourself, Ms. Macy?" He had taken to calling her that soon after she had first arrived.

"It was an adventure, Joseph. You must join us the next time." Making herself comfortable she hoped there would be a next time.

"Hello Joseph. It's nice to see you," Jordan said, shaking his friend's hand.

"Hello, Mr. Jordan. You are looking exceptionally well." Joseph smiled at Jordan. Joseph had always been very observant.

That was one of the reasons that Jordan had hired him. He had no doubt about what was going through the old man's mind.

They rode to the house in the same silence that had plagued them on the plane. For all that they had shared in Pizzolungo, simple conversation seemed alien to them now. As they approached the house they both experienced fluttering stomachs and racing hearts.

Joseph opened the door for Jordan, but when he went to help Macy out of the car Jordan signaled for him to get the bags. Jordan took Macy's hand and helped her out of the car. When they stood facing each other he looked into her eyes. He thought he saw a glimmer of fear. Could she possibly be as nervous as he was? Could she be having the same doubts that he was? Well, somebody had to put an end to it.

He had liked the smiling, attentive Macy that he had known in Sicily a lot better than this timid, quiet person who had shared the journey home with him. He bent down to place a soft seductive kiss on her lips. The smile she bestowed on him put that big yellow thing in the sky to shame.

They walked into the house hand-in-hand to a cheerful Emma, who hugged both of them a million times and chatted on and on about how happy she was to see them. Apparently she and Joseph had already conspired about what had taken place in Sicily.

Jordan was happy that Macy felt so at home now. Emma had marched her right upstairs to take a warm bath as she explained that she had cooked a big pot of spaghetti and meatballs in honor of their return. Jordan smiled to himself as he watched them disappear at the top of the stairs.

She hadn't rejected staying there, and he wondered if she would still want separate rooms. Even if she did, he would not allow it. He went through his mail and listened to an account of the phone messages from Joseph. But he was mentally wishing he could be upstairs enjoying the bath with Macy. Finally, unable to control his longing for her, Jordan put his hand up to stop Joseph's incessant chatter and went upstairs. Noting that her bags had been put in the Peach Room, he sighed with disappointment. He could smell the soft vanilla scent coming from her bathroom and walked into the room. Macy was covered to her neck in thick foamy bubbles. She looked like a little girl with her hair piled on top of her head and her cheeks flushed from the heat.

"I see you are enjoying being pampered by Emma," Jordan said huskily. The sight of her was wreaking havoc on his hormones. He wondered if it would always be this way with them.

She opened one eye to peek at him. "It's wonderful. Would you care to join me, *senor*?" She propped one leg on the side of the tub, dripping water onto the floor.

"I fear that Emma would have me whipped if I did. Although . . ." he said slowly as he traced the bottom of her slender foot, " . . . the offer is appealing."

Macy felt warm all over, and not because of the temperature of the water. Jordan would always be able to evoke that reaction in her. His hand dipped into the water as he rubbed the inside of her thigh. She opened her eyes to see that his were now closed. His fingers explored the place that he had become so familiar with. Macy moaned in pleasure. He bent down to kiss her, to taste the sweetness of her mouth. He rained light kisses on her cheek, her ear. "I will have your things moved into my room. I have no intention of sleeping alone again," he whispered softly into her ear.

Though lost in the sensations that he was reviving in her, what he said quickly registered in her mind.

"Jordan, that room is horrible! I don't want to stay in there," she said adamantly.

"What do you mean horrible?" He frowned at her admission.

"I mean it's so cold and forbidding in there. It's not comfortable at all." He looked perplexed. He had never considered his room cold and forbidding. But he would do anything to have her with him.

"Well, why don't you redecorate it to your liking?"

"Really! I could do that?" she said, almost squealing with excitement. Jordan was pleased.

"Yes, you can do that. But no pink stuff and definitely no flowers. A man's got standards, you know," he said standing up with his hands on his hips. Macy stood up in the tub with bubbles and water dripping onto the peach rugs that lined the floor. She hugged him tightly and placed a sloppy kiss on his mouth.

"Thank you, Jordan. I'll get started right away." Jordan swiped at the bubbles that were dripping from her breasts and watched as the obedient nipple puckered for him.

"I don't think you'll be doing any decorating for at least a couple of hours, *Bella*." He lifted her from the tub and laid her on the peach rug.

CHAPTER FOURTEEN

Time was passing quickly. Jordan had begun shooting his next line of commercials for Jade's new fall colors, which starred Beverly Antill. Beverly was a gorgeous six-foot, dark skinned beauty with romantic green eyes. Needless to say Macy was having a hard time dealing with his co-star. The sultry actress was all but throwing herself at him during the eight-to-ten hours that they were taping each day, and Macy had to admit she felt more than a little threatened by her. No matter how many times Jordan reaffirmed his affection for her, the situation still made Macy nervous. Finally she decided, to Jordan's disappointment, that she would no longer go to the set with him. It was better this way.

She did have her own life; she couldn't just spend all her time with him, no matter how much she wanted to. She knew it wasn't healthy for a relationship anyway. Her career had been on the back burner for months now, and she wondered if it was time she got back to work.

The partners had been pleased with the results of the copyright lawsuit; negotiations were underway for a small out-of-court settlement with the company that had sued Jordan. So with that out of the way she merely reviewed all contracts for the company before anything was signed and sat around the house with Emma and Joseph. But when she'd mentioned going back to work to Jordan, he informed her that he had already taken care of that — he'd spoken with Max Banks soon after they had returned from Sicily. She didn't know exactly what they had talked about, but Jordan had informed her that she'd be working from the house for the time being.

This had given her the time to pursue another hobby of hers, decorating. Since Jordan had given her the okay to redecorate his room she had taken over the whole house. His one request was that she not disturb the room with his weaponry showcase. Macy agreed, mostly because she didn't like going in there anyway. Her latest project was the living room.

"Macy, does everything have to be changed?" Preparing to leave one morning Jordan questioned her about the decorating.

"Yes, because when you decorated you were a lonely bachelor and it showed in your choice of furniture and accessories. Now you're happier and much more content with your life. Besides you need to brighten this place up a bit and people need to know that a woman lives here too," she said as she flipped through another furniture catalog.

"You mean people like Beverly Antill?" Jordan smiled slyly.

"Beverly Antill will not be stepping foot into this house so there's no need to impress her." Macy rolled her eyes.

"Now, now, I just invited her to dinner yesterday." Jordan toyed with one of her books idly.

"Jordan! I know you did no such thing. I swear if she comes in to this house I'll scream!" Macy yelled at him.

"Why Macy, if I didn't know any better I'd think you were jealous." Jordan tried unsuccessfully to hide a snicker.

Macy heard the laughter in his voice and reigned in her temper. She *was not* jealous. Or at least she had no intention of letting him know that she was jealous. "If you knew any better you'd quit while you were ahead." Grabbing her books she prepared to stalk out of the room. Jordan grabbed her at her waist.

"No, no, don't leave, *Bella*." He pulled her close to him and cupped her face in his hands. "You can do whatever you want. This is your home too." He had said that to her frequently over the past few months yet they had never talked of marriage. She didn't even know if he wanted kids or not. They were so close yet still so far apart.

Macy knew that she needed to sit him down and pinpoint where their relationship was going, or not going, but she hadn't had the guts to do so yet. What if she didn't get the answer she wanted? Then she'd have no choice but to leave. And that was the last thing she wanted to do.

"I may be a little late tonight. They want to do some promo shots so don't wait to eat dinner and don't go anywhere without Joseph or Emma." He had given her the same instructions for the last two weeks during which she hadn't been accompanying him to the set. She knew that he still thought of Vincent kidnapping her, and she hated that he felt so bad about it. It wasn't his fault, and there was nothing more he could have done besides rescue her as he did. Still she respected his feelings and obeyed his wishes. She had been complying a lot as of late, but that was required when one was in a serious relationship. And she truly hoped that she and Jordan were in a serious relationship.

After Jordan had left for the day she pushed those thoughts from her mind and went into the room he had designated as her office in an attempt to get some work done. She'd made a call to the office and gotten the number to the opposing attorney in the lawsuit. One of the secretary's had faxed her a copy of the Supplemental Complaint along with a letter outlining what they required to settle the case. The list was extensive, and Macy spent most of the morning going over the pros and cons of it.

Around noon, Emma had brought her a sandwich and she had decided to take a much-needed break. Besides, she needed to talk to Jordan before considering any of the settlement options she had come up with.

After lunch, she ventured into the living room to pick up where she had left off yesterday. Decorating had always been a hobby of hers and now she was thrilled with the opportunity to expand on her ideas. Her morning having been dedicated to contracts and figures, she now stood in the living room furiously fighting with curtains that refused to stay on their hooks. "Damnit!" She missed the hoop and the hook flew across the room.

"A person could get killed in here." Paris dodged the sharp metal object just seconds before would have scraped his face.

"I'm sorry. It's taking a while to get domesticated." Macy smiled at the familiar face.

Paris had become a frequent visitor at the house since his return from Sicily. Although he feigned an interest in the redecorating project, Macy knew the truth. He had become nice to have around, like the brother she never had. He watched her as closely as Jordan did. They both seemed to be afraid that the situation with Vincent was not completely over. She had been meaning to question him about it and now was her chance.

"Have you heard anything from Sicily, Paris?" Retrieving the hook from across the room she inserted it and reached for another one.

"No. Why do you ask?" Stumbling over his words Paris offered her another hook.

"I was just curious. Jordan still seems to have his guard up and he doesn't want me to go anywhere alone."

"He's just concerned about you that's all. I haven't heard anything new. Has Jordan said anything to make you think something's still going on?" Nervously he helped Macy onto the chair that she had placed in front of the window.

Stretching to place the curtains on the rod she continued, "No. I was just wondering. He hardly talks about it now, but sometimes I can tell he's thinking about it."

Macy let the subject drop, recognizing that Paris wasn't going to tell her anything new and continued with the completion of the living room. Paris was quiet for the rest of the afternoon. He usually stayed for dinner when he was there but this time he said he had a previous appointment and almost ran out the door. He was acting really strangely.

Macy ate dinner with Emma in her room while they watched *Pretty Woman*. They enjoyed watching movies together or just talking sometimes. Emma was good company. But tonight she seemed distracted. She wasn't laughing at the parts of the movie that Macy knew were her favorites.

"Emma, are you feeling okay?" Macy asked her finally.

"Me? Yes, I'm fine." Emma said.

"Well, you don't seem to be paying much attention to the movie. I know we've watched it a lot this week but you always enjoy it so much. Is everything alright with Joseph?" Macy had kept the secret of Emma and Joseph's relationship from Jordan. Emma didn't feel that it was appropriate, since they worked together, so Macy had agreed to keep it from Jordan. Not that she thought he would mind, but out of respect for Emma and Joseph she had obliged.

"I was just wondering about something?" Emma said.

"About what?"

"About when you were planning to tell Mr. Jordan that you're having a baby?" Macy almost fainted on the spot. She had tried so hard to keep any of the signs from showing. In the mornings when she was sick she would go to the bathroom down the hall so that Jordan wouldn't hear her. But it seems that she was only successful in fooling one person. Herself. How long had she thought she could go without telling someone? How long had she wanted to go without telling someone?

"Oh, Emma. I've been trying so hard not to think about it lately. I didn't know who I could talk to." She began to cry.

"Hush, now. You can always talk to Emma. I won't tell Mr. Jordan, that's your place. But you should have told me. I need to take special care of you now." Emma had come over to the chair where Macy sat and hugged her close to her ample bosom. "You're not the first one to have doubts about having a baby Ms. Macy. Everything will be just fine."

"Oh no, you don't understand. I want this baby more than I've ever wanted anything in my life, but I don't know that Jordan will feel the same. I don't even know if he wants kids," Macy sniffled.

"Well, you know, I can't say. He's never had any nieces or nephews and I've never seen him with a child, but he's different now that he's with you. He's happy now. I'm sure he'll be happy about his baby too."

"But, I want to get married and have a family. A real family. I'm afraid that Jordan won't understand that in light of how he grew up." Macy had shared the story of Jordan's childhood with Emma one night so she understood exactly what she meant.

"Do you love him?" Emma asked her as she took a tissue out of her pocket and wiped Macy's face.

"Yes, I love him so much it hurts," Macy said.

"Then you have to trust him," was all Emma said before they both heard the front door signaling Jordan's return home. "I'll go see to him. You get yourself together." Macy sat in the room staring blankly at the screen. Richard Gere was rescuing Julia Roberts from the tower. She'd thought of Jordan as her rescuer, but now she was afraid that she had screwed up her own fairy tale.

"Where is Macy, Emma?" She could hear him before she saw him.

"I'm right here, baby," She said as calmly as she could.

"Where were you? Are you okay?" Jordan hovered over her as she reclined in the chair. Intense eyes watched her as she sat up in the chair.

"I'm fine. I just dozed off in Emma's room. We were watching *Pretty Woman*, again." Trying to smile she stared up at him.

"You women and that movie. You look tired. Why don't you go on up to bed." Stroking her hair absently, he noted the stressful look on her face and thought she may have been crying. Macy was glad he had suggested she go upstairs. She needed to get away from him. He was watching her too closely and she was definitely not ready to tell him about the baby.

"Yeah, I think I'll do that. You'll be up soon?" She asked as she approached the steps.

"I sure will. Save my spot," he said smiling.

"I will." She walked up the steps feeling the weight of the world on her shoulders. He knew something was wrong, she could tell. She just prayed he wouldn't press her for an answer tonight.

"Did something happen today, Emma?" Jordan followed Emma into the kitchen to get something to eat.

"No. Mr. Jordan. We had a good day. Ms. Macy hung those curtains and Mr. Paris came to see her. We had lunch together and then she was in the living room moving things around. I think she's just tired like you said." Emma talked as she moved around hoping that Jordan would believe her.

"How long was Paris here?" Jordan mentally noted that Paris always seemed to visit when he wasn't around.

"About two hours. He stayed in the living room with Ms. Macy the whole time, but he didn't stay for dinner like he usually does.

Maybe he knew you wouldn't be home." Emma continued to talk as she placed a sandwich in front of Jordan.

"Did I get any calls today?"

"No sir. Were you expecting someone to call?"

"No, not especially." Emma left Jordan in the kitchen. He sat at the table and stared at the sandwich for a long time. On the set today he had looked up and seen a man who looked strangely enough like Matthew. Matthew was dead. That idea wasn't possible. Nevertheless it had startled him and he had been unable to concentrate all afternoon.

And now he came home and Macy was acting strange. She looked a little pale. He hoped she wasn't sick. He should go up and check on her.

He walked into the bedroom and flicked on a lamp by the bed. It shone brightly against the navy blue comforter that Macy had picked out to match the new slate blue walls and carpet. He had to admit that the room was a little more comforting now. It had a sort of lived in look. She was curled up on her side of the bed looking lost in all the covers and pillows she liked so much.

"Macy?" He said softly. Wiping stray tendrils of hair away from her face he saw that she was asleep. He wouldn't wake her. He took a shower and got into bed with her, cradling her in his arms: Lying there, he thought of how important she was to him and how he would do anything to protect her. She briefly stirred and shifted her position. Her soft breathing ruffled the hairs on his chest as she resumed her slumber. Jordan fell asleep thinking of how lucky he was to have her.

It had taken some time but he had succeeded in getting a job on the set so that he could be closer to Jordan. An accidental death would look better than another murder. He hadn't meant for Jordan to see him so soon but that was okay too. He had scared him pretty damn good. He had followed him home so that he could find out about his security and things of that nature.

Jordan had never had security before but he would want to protect his little woman now. He hadn't gotten a glance of her as he walked around peeping through the windows but he did see the back entrance that had been left unlocked. He would just walk around and get a better view of things while he was there.

The kitchen was dark and quiet. He assumed that Emma and Joseph were fast asleep. He took the stairs two at a time, his footsteps muffled by the thick carpet. He knew exactly which room was Jordan's. He approached it slowly and saw Macy sleeping quietly. He heard the water running in the bathroom and assumed that Jordan would be joining her shortly. She was a pretty little thing. When the water had been shut off he crept out of the room.

As he wandered through the house, he had an idea to further his revenge on Jordan. He circled through the living room and back into the kitchen. Finding the door that led downstairs, he set out for Jordan's weaponry room in search of an old pistol that he had been especially proud of obtaining. After lighting a kerosene lamp, he located it and gently took it off the wall to have a closer look. An engraved Colt 45 manufactured in 1917. Bright nickel and gold shimmered in his hand. He fingered the Texas Ranger emblem and smiled.

He wouldn't need this much longer, and he remembered the price Jordan had paid for it four years ago. It had to be worth almost triple that amount now - another incentive to his plan. As he turned to leave the room he accidentally knocked over the lamp. He knew that it would be only moments before someone came into the room to investigate so he decided not to try and put out the small fire that had ignited. He left the house the same way he had come in.

At the sound of a crash, Jordan was awake instantly. His jolting motion awakened Macy as well.

"What's the matter?" she asked groggily.

"Nothing. You stay here. Do you hear me? Don't move!" Grabbing his robe he raced out of the room. Macy's heart was pounding. What was going on?

Ignoring Jordan's directions, she got out of bed and followed him down the steps.

"Mr. Jordan! Mr. Jordan! Someone was here!!" Yelling, Emma ran into the hallway meeting Jordan before he could enter the room where Joseph was placing damp towels over the small fire on the floor.

"Get some flashlights Emma," Jordan ordered.

"What do you think Joseph?" Jordan asked as he surveyed the room. It didn't look like a burglary attempt but you could never be too sure.

"Somebody was definitely in here," Joseph said sadly.

"How do you know? Is something missing?" Jordan asked.

"No, not that I can tell, but I watered the grass late this evening so it's still a little damp especially near the new bushes I planted."

"Joseph, what does that have to do with anything?" Emma was asking as she returned with the flashlights.

"Well, there were footprints in the kitchen and they lead into the hallway near the steps." Joseph looked at Jordan knowingly.

Jordan had told Joseph what had taken place in Sicily and had shared his concerns for Macy and any attempts at retaliation.

Jordan felt sick. Fear lodged in his chest. Either Vincent had gotten out of jail or the other man Macy had heard at the cabin had come to finish the job.

"Jordan, what's going on?" Macy came into the room.

"Macy, I told you to stay put, didn't I? You shouldn't be down here," he yelled.

"Well, I wanted to make sure you were alright," she said as the tears spilled from her eyes. This pregnancy thing was making her a weeping well. She turned and rushed out of the room. Emma mumbled something and followed her.

"First thing tomorrow morning you get a security system installed Joseph. Macy is not to be let out of your sight. Do you understand?" Jordan glared at Joseph.

Joseph, understanding his employer's unspoken emotions, nodded his head in compliance.

"Yes sir. What about you Mr. Jordan?"

"What about me?"

"Won't he come after you too? Who will protect you if I'm watching Macy?" Joseph asked seriously, his tall thin form stood tensely in the small room.

"I'll protect myself." Jordan turned to continue his survey of the room. It was gone. The Texas Ranger Colt 45 that he'd paid forty-five hundred dollars for was gone.

Maybe it had been just a burglary after all, he thought. But why come all the way down here to take something when there were so many valuable things upstairs. Unless the burglar already knew what he wanted.

"Sir, I would like to recommend an excellent bodyguard. He has worked for many well-known people in the past and I myself would feel better if I knew you had some solid protection. I'll call him in the morning. You don't leave the house until he gets here," Joseph quickly walked past Jordan. " And I do not wish to hear another word about it," he yelled over his shoulder with finality.

Joseph had been with him for ten years and he was very fond of the old man. He also understood his protective instincts. That was the reason that he didn't bother to argue with him. He would wait for the bodyguard to appease Joseph.

Upstairs Macy lay across the bed crying with Emma rubbing her back. She wasn't even exactly sure why she was crying. Jordan had yelled at her but she'd known he would. She just felt so overwhelmed. She knew that Jordan was afraid; she was afraid herself. But she was pregnant, and Jordan didn't know that. And now, someone had broken into the house and started a fire. So much was going on, her mind reeled from it.

"Ms. Macy, you have to tell Mr. Jordan. Something strange is going on here and we need to be prepared for whatever happens. He has to know the truth," Emma urged her. Macy knew that she was right. She knew that this break-in was connected to what had happened in Sicily, and she owed it to Jordan as well as their unborn child to protect herself.

"What truth must I know?" Jordan had entered the room without either of the women noticing. Macy's head snapped up, she saw the anger building in him. The last thing she wanted was to deal with him at this moment, but she knew she had no choice.

"I'll go downstairs and make you some warm milk. Would you like some Mr. Jordan?" Moving to the door Emma waited for his response.

"No thank you, Emma." He answered without taking his eyes off Macy.

"I'll make you some too, you're gonna need it." Emma patted

his shoulder before leaving the room. Jordan stared at Emma's descending back, wondering when he had lost control of his household.

"Macy, is there something I should know?" he requested as calmly as he could. She began to cry again. He was confused. Macy was not acting like herself. Why wasn't she arguing with him about him yelling at her? What was going on?

"Oh, Jordan, I'm so sorry. You never said you didn't want children, and I didn't know. You remember that first time don't you? I was so scared when I found out, but now I want our baby and you can't make me get rid of it!" She sat in the middle of the bed yelling.

"Our baby? You're pregnant?" Things began to fall into place now. He sat on the bed as his mind unraveled the second mystery of the night. Macy was pregnant. She was having his baby. This was turning out to be one eventful evening.

"Yes." She watched him trying to figure out his reaction.

"I can't believe this. How far along are you?" He asked stunned and holding his head in his hands.

"Twelve weeks."

"Twelve weeks! When were you going to tell me?" Staring at her in disbelief, Jodan felt a headache coming on.

"I don't know. You never said if you wanted children or not and we never talked about it, so I wasn't sure. I didn't want you to be mad." Taking a deep breath she took a chance and looked at him.

"I would not . . . I am not mad, Macy. I can't think of anyone else I'd rather have my child than you. Is it what you want?" He asked cautiously, not wanting to upset her anymore and still not clear on how she felt about the pregnancy.

"Yes, it's what I want. I mean, I want to have a family and I love you, so I guess you're the one I'll have a family with. Is that what you want?" She was afraid of the answer, but relieved that she'd finally know where their relationship was going.

"I know that I've been reluctant to tell you exactly how I've been feeling lately." Jordan sat on the bed and pulled her onto his lap.

"Well you can tell me now," she said wrapping her arms around his neck.

"It just feels so right to come home and find you here, to go to bed and have you next to me. When you redecorated the room, I felt even closer to you and when you began to redecorate the whole house, I figured you were making it your home too. I've been alone for so long that it seems almost foreign to me to have to tell someone what I'm feeling. I should have told you that I wanted to marry you sooner. It shouldn't have taken your getting pregnant for me to say that to you."

"You want to get married?"

"Remember, I told you that fate had brought us together. I knew from the moment I saw you that we were meant for each other. And I will never love anyone as I love you. It has always been my plan to marry you." He kissed her then, slowly and completely as she gradually began to relax.

"I was so afraid."

"I know and I apologize. It was my fault. But you have to be patient with me. As I said I'm not used to sharing all my feelings with anyone. But I want us to share everything Macy. Everything. Do you understand? No more secrets?"

"No more secrets." Jordan placed his hand on her stomach. She was having his baby. It was unbelievable. How could his love life be going along so right while his family life was falling apart.

"Um, Jordan there is something else."

"What else Macy?" He was sure nothing could take the joy he

felt right now away from him.

"Well, when Paris was here earlier, I asked him if he had heard anything more from Sicily, and he started acting really strangely. He practically ran out of here. I just thought it was weird, you know, his reaction and all." She replayed the scene in her mind. Jordan listened. He, too, had been thinking that Paris was acting strangely since his return to the States. He usually loved being on the set when Jordan was filming, but when Macy had stopped coming, so did Paris. And it seemed that he would always stop by the house when Jordan wasn't home.

CHAPTER FIFTEEN

The press had done its job again. There were articles in every tabloid known to man about Jordan Blake, his mistress and the threat to their lives. Because of his father, it was commonly assumed that it was mafia related or worse, a drug deal gone badly. Jordan wondered why they always came up with the worst-case scenario first.

Macy had been extremely distraught when she was named in one of the magazines. She wasn't sure what it would do to her career in the long run. Jordan had assured her that the firm would stand behind her, but she was still pretty shaken up about it. The whole situation was stressing her out. She worried about Jordan. She worried about the baby. It seemed that all she did now was worry.

After the break-in a security system had been installed at the house and a guard was with Jordan as well as with Macy at all times. The impact of the impending danger that surrounded them was encompassing their lives. Todd Burns was with Macy all day. Although he was out of sight most of the time, she still knew he was close by. When she and Emma went to the market or when she had a doctor's appointment, he was right there.

It wasn't as bad for Jordan. He rarely even noticed Michael Tandan, whom Joseph had employed to guard him during working hours. He had spoken to Michael and they had decided that it was more probable that whoever was behind all this would try to orchestrate an accident on the set as opposed to a direct hit on Jordan.

Where Macy was concerned, however, Jordan believed that they would try another kidnapping as opposed to actually hurting her. Nevertheless, he wanted her protected from any harm, especially in her present condition.

Since finding out that Macy was carrying his child, he had begun to look at his life differently. He was now envisioning his family; his wife, his child or children and their life together. He would no longer be alone in the world. He and Macy had not set a wedding date yet; she was still deciding what she wanted to do. He wasn't even sure if she had told her family. He knew that she was close to them and that this would be a big deal with her being the first to get married and having the first grandchild, but she wasn't saying much about them right now. He had contemplated sending her back to New York until this whole thing was over, but he felt safer knowing that he could get to her quickly should he need to.

Matthew and Vincent sat in the truck across from Jordan's house. They had seen the car pull into the gates a few minutes ago. They assumed that Macy was in the house. Since there was a new alarm system, Matthew had decided not to venture onto the property again. He needed to come up with a better plan.

"Matt, what are we doing?" Vincent bit into his cheeseburger.

"We're thinking, Vinnie. I need to figure out how to get her out of that house. Have you seen Paris?" Matthew asked.

"No. He wasn't at his apartment when I went by last night. You think he told Jordan something?" Vincent bit into the burger again, this time spilling mustard and ketchup onto his pants. "Shit!"

Yelling, he tried to swipe it off his pants without making too much of a mess.

"Nah, he'd be too scared. Besides he couldn't tell anything without admitting that he was involved, and I don't think he wants Jordan to know that, but find him anyway. We're gonna need him. I've decided that I want Jordan and his pretty little woman together in the end. They won't live happily ever after together, but they'll die together, that's good enough." Matthew fingered a white letter sized envelope. "And hurry up with that; you're making a mess!" He yelled at Vinnie.

"What did they have to say this time?" Nodding briefly toward the envelope Vinnie proceeded to devour his half eaten cheese-burger.

"They said he's doing better, but his heart's still not good. Too much stress could do him in for good. And if we don't get Jordan out of the picture pretty damn quick, he's gonna inherit everything."

"Yeah, I know." Vinnie felt a little sadness from deep within him. His father was seriously ill and they were plotting to kill their brother. What kind of life did he have and what kind of life would he have after all was said and done?

A rich one, he decided. His father had no right changing his will to reflect that Jordan would inherit his house, cars, winery and the larger percentage of his fortune. Originally, the house in Sicily had been willed to Vincent – with him being the legal heir — along with sixty percent of the winery. Matthew and Jordan were to split the remaining forty percent of the winery and Theresa would get a sizable chunk of money. Santina would get the villa in Naples.

Then eight years ago he had it changed. Matthew and Vincent were still inheriting a good chunk of money but Jordan would get the business. Theresa would now get the house in Sicily and a good chunk of money. Santina's inheritance hadn't changed.

Either way Matthew and Vincent felt slighted. After all, Jordan had been the one who had refused to have anything to do with Dioncello, while Matthew and Vincent had tried to forge a bond with him.

But Jordan had always been the one. He'd always been the favorite. Maybe because he'd stayed away. In any event it didn't matter, Jordan didn't need the winery nor did he need the money. He had enough of his own.

Matthew and Vincent had long since agreed that Jordan didn't deserve to inherit the Penelli fortune. But it was always Jordan. Dioncello wanted Jordan's forgiveness and he thought that if he couldn't get it while he was alive, he would obtain it through his death. Well, they didn't intend to give Jordan that chance.

Macy hung up the phone and stared at it for a few minutes. In her five-year tenure at the firm she had only seen Maxwell Banks four times and she had only spoken to him once, at her second interview. But today he had called her. He was concerned about her personal relationship with Jordan. Boy, good news traveled fast. Although the tabloids had not gotten wind of her pregnancy, yet, they drew a pretty good picture about what was going on between the two of them. But, why would that matter to Mr. Banks? One would think that with all he did to accommodate Jordan in the beginning, he would be ecstatic that she had managed to ensure that the firm would continue to benefit financially from him. And he had spoken to Jordan soon after their return from Sicily. She had assumed it had been an amiable conversation but she hadn't asked Jordan for any specifics.

Today he'd sounded almost scared for her. She had always had a nagging feeling in the back of her mind about the firm's connection to Jordan and his family. Especially, with their insistence that she move out here with Jordan and that she do everything in her power to keep him happy. Well she thought that was what she had been doing, but Mr. Banks'tone was definitely troubled. He questioned her incessantly about her personal protection as well as Jordan's. This wasn't normal for the firm regardless of how much money the client had.

She remembered hearing at one time that Mr. Banks was married to an Italian woman. Macy wondered if there was a connection between the families. Macy would have to investigate this further. Maybe there was something bigger going on than just a jealous brother.

"Ms. Macy, your appointment is at twelve. You are going aren't you?" Emma gently scooted Macy to the side and continued dusting the table that Macy had been leaning on.

"Oh, yes. Tell Todd that I'll be ready in ten minutes." She went upstairs to wash her face and hands. As she turned off the water she heard the doorbell. She figured it was probably Todd coming in to get her. He never stayed in the house with her, he spent the day keeping watch outside of the house, checking and double-checking the alarms and the windows.

Macy grabbed a light jacket; it would be chilly in the doctor's office. Although she was in L.A. and was not in danger of below zero temperatures as she was in New York, she found that her body was still adjusting to air conditioning all year long, so she took a sweater or jacket whenever she went out. The only problem now was that she and Emma would have to go shopping soon because not only was she bursting out of her petite size eight jeans, but her close cut jackets were cutting a little too close. She would suggest that they go shopping this weekend. That way Jordan could go with her. They rarely went out anymore, and she thought it would be nice for them to spend some time together away from home.

"Macy?" There was a soft knock at the door and then she heard Paris' familiar voice.

"Come in, Paris." She was a little startled that he had come upstairs and into her bedroom. He had never done that before. She hadn't seen him since the last time he had run from the house, before the security systems were installed and before someone had broken into her home.

"I just thought I'd stop by and see how you were doing." He eyed her suspiciously. Macy protectively closed her jacket around her bulging midsection. She wasn't sure why, but she didn't feel that Paris needed to know about the pregnancy just yet.

"I'm fine. Actually, Jordan and I were wondering where you had been. We haven't heard from you in almost a month now." Macy watched him, trying to discern his reaction.

"Well, I've been around. I just got hooked up with this new client and I've been trying to get them out of some pretty serious stuff they're in. You know, I need to expand my business a little. With Jordan having you here now he doesn't need to keep me on his payroll." Macy had never heard him comment on Jordan's retaining her to represent him in the past, so this came as a shock to her, even though it shouldn't have, considering she did take over his job. Paris looked a little jittery, his eyes darting abut the room erratically.

"Paris, you know Jordan still needs you and you're his friend. He values your opinions as much as he values your friendship." Macy moved closer to the door. Paris' shifting eyes and jitteriness concerned her.

"I didn't come here to discuss my job, Macy." The troubled man stood about ten feet away from her as he stuffed his hands into his pockets.

"Well what did you come here for?"

His voice was low, almost a whisper when he said, "To warn you." Macy's racing heart stopped cold.

"What? Warn me? Warn me about what, Paris?" Paris walked over to the window and stared out at the lawn. He saw the truck parked at the bottom of the hill and for the first time in his life he felt fear. Fear for his friend, fear for this woman who had unknowingly gotten involved with the wrong man, and fear for his own life if he did not do what was being asked of him. But when he turned and looked into Macy's shimmering brown eyes etched with the same fear he felt, he knew another feeling. Shame.

How could he do this to the one person who had been there for him all his life, to the best friend he had ever had. He knew how he could. He owed Matthew a great deal of money for the drugs he had supplied him with, but Matthew was willing to forego the debt if he could do this one thing for him. He would do it but he had decided this morning that he would give Macy and Jordan every chance he could to prepare themselves for what was about to happen and possibly give them a chance to escape, which would take a load of guilt off his shoulders.

"I asked you a question Paris?" Macy demanded an answer.

"Macy, I've been reading the papers and I think that you and Jordan should be really careful."

"You know something don't you? Who was it that broke in here?" When Paris didn't answer her she continued. "You do know. Paris, was it . . . was it Vincent? Has he come here to finish what he started in Sicily?" She took a tentative step towards him.

"Oh Macy, it's so much more than you know. But yes, Vincent is here. I'm not sure how he got out of jail but he's here, and I've seen him." Paris shifted from one foot to another anxious to get this over with. His brow was dotted with tiny beads of sweat. Macy's line of questioning grew more intense.

"You've seen him? Where?" The room seemed to spin around her.

"He's been in the house and he's probably watching you right now." Macy grabbed the side of the dresser to balance herself. Luckily it was there or she would have hit the floor. This was not just a man upset with his brother. This was a truly sick man who had followed them across the world and continued to stalk them.

"How do you know this Paris?" She was beginning to get the picture now. Paris was also involved. And if that were the case then why was she still in this room with him? Why didn't she call for help? Because she could see that Paris had no intention of hurting her, almost like Vincent. But Paris didn't look crazy. He looked scared.

"It doesn't matter. I just wanted to tell you that something is in the works. I'm not sure of the details, but you and Jordan need to be on your guard." H walked past her and opened the door. "I can't face Jordan. Please tell him I'm sorry." The room was silent.

"Can you do that for me Macy?" She wouldn't look at him as she turned away from the door; but she heard the torment in his voice. She nodded her head in agreement as she gulped back the tears that were threatening to surface.

"Remember, be very careful Macy. Don't trust anyone but Jordan, do you understand what I'm telling you?" Macy nodded again. Paris reached out his hand to touch her shoulder in comfort, but pulled it back. He had no right to comfort her now.

He brushed past her on his way out the door and she sank to the floor. Tears, hot and wet, streamed down her cheeks and stained the blue jacket she had wrapped around her shoulders.

On the set Jordan was irritable and tired, he knew that Macy had a doctor's appointment today and he was worried about her. He wanted to be home with her instead of on the set, but they were wrapping up the commercial today so he'd have more time to spend with her after it was done.

They had a thirty-minute break for lunch and Jordan rushed to the trailer to call home. As he approached the trailer he saw a man in a dark sweat suit creeping away from the door of the trailer. He started to chase the man but remembered that Michael would be right behind him. Jordan turned to see him signaling that he had seen the man as well.

"I'll check the trailer out first, then I'll try and find him," he said as he walked ahead of Jordan. Jordan waited impatiently while Michael searched the trailer.

"It's fine, but I found this on the table." He handed Jordan a white envelope with a red rose painted on the front of it. "It doesn't feel like there's anything in it besides a letter. Do you want me to read it?" Michael asked.

"No, I'll do it. Just try and find the guy." He watched Michael walk away, stop and then turned back to him. "I know, Tandan. I'll wait inside the trailer until you get back." Jordan was really getting tired of being treated like a sick child. But he knew that it was necessary.

Stepping into the trailer Jordan closed the door behind him. He looked around the small room and noted that nothing had been disturbed. He sat down and fingered the envelope. The rose was intricately drawn and painted a deep red. Jordan didn't have to guess at who had sent the letter. His mother had always loved roses. She had them planted all around their little house in Connecticut, in all different colors. She loved the smell of them and how they were so faithful, returning year after year.

Jordan,

You've been a busy boy haven't you? Why didn't you tell me I was going to be an uncle? Well I guess you couldn't tell me since you believed me to be dead. If you could have seen your face when I showed up on the set, I wish I had a picture of that moment. You're probably trying to figure out what's going on and I believe it's time to bring this to a close. So I've decided to make it easy for you. I want you to meet me at the Sandstone Garage at 9 p.m. Saturday night and bring that pretty little woman of yours with you. Don't you think I should meet my future sister-in-law? Don't bring any - one else with you! This includes your bodyguard and Macy's as well. I will know if someone else comes with you Jordan and I warn you, you won't like the repercussions your disobedience will bring.

Matt

Jordan folded the letter and neatly placed it back into the envelope. He sat in the chair and once again stared fixedly at the flower on the envelope. What was going on? For the life of him he could not figure this out. He and Matthew had always had a good relationship with each other as well as their mother, even though Jordan was smart enough to know that things weren't always what they seemed. And Matthew, it appeared, was not the loving son and brother that he had believed him to be.

So he and Vincent were partners. That, more than likely, was the second male voice Macy had heard at the cottage. What would make a man commit murder? Money. That was the only logical answer. Jordan's company was at the top in its game, and his clothing line was taking off, so he realized that he did have the kind of money that someone would kill for, but his mother hadn't; so this situation got more confusing as each day passed. There had to be something else. *Dioncello*. His connection could be the answer.

CHAPTER SIXTEEN

Macy had been a nervous wreck since Paris had left. She had Emma cancel her doctor's appointment for fear of leaving the house, even if Todd and Emma would accompany her. She had stayed in her bedroom for the remainder of the day waiting for Jordan to come home. Emma had brought her lunch up to her and asked her a million questions. Macy assured her that she was fine, that she was just tired, but Emma knew that there was something else going on.

Afraid that her panic would overtake her, Macy called her mother and they talked for over an hour. She was filled in on her sister's grades and new boyfriend and her mother's new addition to the house and her bridge club. It made Macy feel better to hear about something else other than her troubles. Her mother waited until the very end of the conversation to ask her about Jordan. It seems she had also read about what was going on. She was concerned but she knew that Macy was stubborn, and even if she begged her she would not come home.

Macy reassured her mother that she was fine and that Jordan was taking very good care of her. She promised that they would visit as soon as Jordan finished with the promotions for the fall line. She neglected to tell her that she was pregnant. She knew it was a mistake not to because it was only a matter of time before the media got wind of that information as well, but she didn't want to overly stress her mother. And besides, she knew her mother well;

she would have been on the next plane to L.A. to collect her daughter and unborn grandchild.

After talking to her mother and taking a soothing bubble bath she lay across the bed and tried to concentrate on some contracts she needed to review. It was amazing how much women paid for a tube of lipstick and eyeliner these days. And Jordan's popularity was soaring right along with his profit margin. There was an offer to pose for Playgirl, a local college wanted him to pose for their calendar, and various other functions that she needed to weed through and sort out. Her unborn child sensed the tension in its mother and beckoned for her to take a nap.

She awoke to a gentle stroking along her back and warm kisses on her cheek. She knew exactly who the culprit was and opened her eyes to greet him.

"Hello." Bringing his face into full focus she smiled at him.

"Hello to you. How are you?" Jordan stroked the spot on her cheek that he had just kissed. She had looked so peaceful lying there sound asleep. He hated what he had to tell her knowing that her serenity would be shattered.

"I'm fine. How about you?" She asked sitting up so that she now sat in front of him on the king sized bed they shared.

"I'm better now that I'm home with you. Emma mentioned that you canceled your doctor's appointment. What happened?" Concern wrinkled his brow; he knew how important it was for a woman to receive the proper pre-natal care.

"Paris came by just as I was getting ready to leave. He said some things that upset me." She fiddled with the gold embroidery on the comforter.

"What did he say?" Seeing the change in Jordan's eyes she shifted beneath the heavy blanket, suddenly uncomfortable.

"He came to warn us." Her bottom lip trembled as the words

came out. Jordan hugged her close to him as she wept. He waited patiently while she calmed down sensing that she had been holding that in all day.

"Did he say anything else?" Closing his eyes to the pain her tears brought him, Jordan cradled her head against his chest.

"He said to tell you he was sorry. Jordan, Vincent's back and he was in the house and he's been watching us and . . ." She was rambling. Jordan smoothed her hair and rocked her like a baby.

"Shhh. It's okay, *Bella*. It's okay. I know he's back." He knew that he should tell her everything, but how could he upset her more than she already was.

But hadn't he said no more secrets; he had to abide by his own rule.

"*Bella*, I need you to listen to me carefully." He waited again for her to calm down. Once she felt in control of her emotions again, she pulled away to look at Jordan.

"What is it? You're not telling me something." She said. He held her hands in his and stared down at their petite exquisiteness. He kissed each finger one by one before he began.

"I want to first apologize." Dark eyes watched her closely. Macy marveled at how beautiful he was and wondered briefly, if she should have a male child, would he look like his father.

"Apologize? For what?" She asked putting thoughts of their unborn child aside for the moment.

"For involving you in my mess. You had absolutely nothing to do with this and I pulled you into it. I should have just let you stay in New York instead of insisting that you come here." Jordan's shoulders slumped as he finally vocalized the guilt he had been carrying for the past few months.

"I'm kind of glad you insisted that I come. How would I have ever found you had I stayed in New York and you stayed in L.A."

Macy gave him a little smile in an attempt to lighten the mood. It didn't work.

"You are so important to me. Six months ago I wouldn't care about Vincent or Paris or any of this, but now things are different. I have so much to lose now." He brought her hands up to caress his face.

"You won't lose me Jordan. We'll get through this. I know we will."

"You are so unbelievable. Even in your own fear you find the strength to console me. You have one terrific mother, little one," Jordan said as he rubbed his hand across her belly, glorying in the slight bulge that he felt. His heart was so full of love for this woman and his child.

Taking a deep breath he began with his news, "Matthew is still alive. He apparently faked his own death. His was the other voice you heard that morning at the cottage. He left this in my trailer today." Handing her the note he lay back against the pillows while she read it.

"Why?"

"I don't know." Pain seared through him as he admitted his own confusion. "Matthew and I were always together. We were as close as two brothers could be. I just don't know when things changed."

"Do you think he was responsible for your mother as well?" Macy hadn't wanted to ask the question, but she knew the same thought had to have crossed his mind.

"I don't know. A part of me wants to believe he could never do such a thing, but I don't think I know who Matt is anymore." Taking a deep breath he added, "I don't think I ever knew who he was."

"He's as crazy as Vincent. What is it that they want from you?" Slamming the paper down on the bed she turned to him.

"I don't think they want anything from me. I think my very

existence is problematic for them in some way. I mean, isn't the undertone of jealousy and resentment obvious? I don't know. Every time I think I have it all figured out something else comes up and throws me for a loop. Now Paris seems to be involved too. I just don't know Macy. I don't know who to trust anymore."

"You can trust me." Lying next to him she took his hand in hers. They lay there both lost in their own thoughts, Macy thinking about when they first met and how she resisted the attraction between them, and Jordan thinking about their time at the cottage in Sicily and how he wished things could have stayed that simple.

He raised himself up on his elbow and looked down into her eyes. The eyes that he had come to love. In them he saw all the emotion she felt for him and it was overwhelming. He bent down and touched his lips to hers. The contact was instantly electrifying. They surrendered helplessly to the passion that now ruled their body and soul completely.

He still reveled in how much she could excite him with little or no effort. When Jordan removed her gown and found that she had worn no underwear he thought he would explode with need. She moaned at his touch and wriggled beneath him as he attempted to remove his clothes without ending their contact.

Entering her slowly and without preamble Macy shuddered with the intense stream of emotions that flowed through her. They engaged in a smooth gentle rhythm whispering their love for one another and enjoying the connection that had brought them so far.

Jordan's mind began to blur at the sleek wetness that engulfed him. Warm muscles contracted constantly bringing his engorged sex to a hardness that he had never experienced before.

His motions above her had Macy squirming beneath him as the head of his penis slipped gently in and out of her. Clasping her legs around his waist she gave him unlimited access. Holding his buttocks she ensured her ultimate pleasure.

Panting and sweating, moaning and whispering, they climbed the mountain and jumped into the abyss of their love.

It was late evening when Jordan went to the kitchen to find something to eat for them both. Emma had cooked a dish that resembled beef and vegetables and rice of some kind. It smelled good and that was enough for him.

Macy, of course, would eat it gladly. He envisioned her having to be carted around by her seventh month of pregnancy. She had already possessed a pretty healthy appetite without the extra person added, so she was bound to gain lots of weight. He found himself looking forward to it.

"Hmmmm. That smells good. What is it?" Walking into the kitchen just as Jordan removed the dish from the microwave, she stood beside him at the counter.

"I'm not sure. But like you said it smells good." They carried their plates and drinks into the newly decorated family room. Macy's idea of course. She wanted a room for them to sit in and relax together. Preferably one that didn't have a bed; not that that mattered; two mornings ago in the shower could attest to that. They ate and watched TV, both refusing to speak about Vincent and Matthew.

But returning to their room and lying in the darkness the inevitable could not be denied.

CHAPTER SEVENTEEN

Macy awoke early the next morning with Jordan. She had planned a meeting in the city that might shed some light on their problems. She needed to know what Maxwell Banks' involvement was. She was still a little nervous about leaving the house, but she would have Todd and Emma with her. She did trust both of them no matter what Paris said. She lay across the bed and watched Jordan as he dressed in blue jeans and a black silk T-shirt that molded and sculpted his well-toned body. He was so damn sexy. She couldn't blame Playgirl for wanting him or anyone else for that matter.

"What are you staring at?" He smiled at her through the floor length mirror.

"Oh, nothing. Just taking stock of my investment."

"Your investment?" Buckling his belt, he turned to face her.

"Yeah, if I'm going to spend the rest of my life with you, I have to make sure you're fit for the job." She smiled.

"Oh, I think I can handle it. The question is can you?" He scooped her up off the bed and held her in his arms.

"I guess you'll do." She laughed as he hugged her closer to him and nuzzled her neck.

He released her slightly until her feet could touch the floor, then kissed her forehead and turned to put on his shoes.

"Call the doctor and reschedule that appointment for as soon as possible, I don't want you neglecting your health or the baby's. Okay?" He said over his shoulder.

"I will."

"What are you going to do today?" She couldn't lie to him but she wouldn't tell him the whole truth.

"I was thinking of going shopping. I kind of outgrew most of my things. Emma will go with me I'm sure," she said absently. She didn't notice the brief look of panic that crossed Jordan's face. But she did recognize the silence.

"Jordan, I'll be fine. Todd will be with me too."

"You be very careful. I'll give Todd, Matthew and Vincent's description on my way out, but you take care of your business and come right back home. Understand?"

"Jordan, I am not a child. How many times do we have to go through this?

"As many as it takes for you to understand. I don't want you hurt, Macy. I know that I can't be with you to protect you every second of every day, nor can I expect you to be a prisoner in your own home. But I do expect you to take all necessary precautions for yourself as well as our child. Now, we will not compromise on this. You will go shopping, purchase the things you need and come home. I'll call to check on you."

"Anything else, Master?" She teased.

"No pouting. You're much too beautiful to pout." He cupped her face and kissed her thoroughly. "I love you so much, *Bella*." Desperation etched his voice.

"I know. I love you too, Jordan. I promised you we would get through this and we will, you'll see. But for now I will go shopping and come right back. I think I'll buy some sexy lingerie and try and seduce my man tonight. Don't you think that sounds good?" Her hand moved to his zipper.

"I think that feels wonderful. I'll hurry home," he said and pulled away from her while he still had the wits to do so.

After he was gone Macy dressed in sweat pants and a thick sweatshirt. She looked into the mirror and could hardly tell that she was four and a half months pregnant. She hoped that no one else could tell either. After she had eaten a hearty breakfast of scrambled eggs with cheese, bacon, toast and grapefruit, she went out on the terrace to water the roses that seemed to engulf the house. She didn't see Todd but she knew he was around. She had heard Emma talking to him while she ate. After watering the flowers she realized that she was just a little tired. Being pregnant was taking all her energy. She sat in the chair and watched the light breeze blowing through the trees. Closing her eyes she relaxed for a moment before her thoughts were interrupted by a sound. She looked in the direction it had come from and saw a flash of white disappear behind a tree.

Her heart hammered in her chest. She watched that same spot for a few more minutes before she began to calm down. She was being paranoid. She rose to go into the house when she spotted an envelope on the ledge. She let out a gasp. It had not been there when she came out of the house, which meant someone had just been there. Had just been that close to her, but hadn't harmed her.

Macy,

I am so sorry for scaring you this way. It's Matt's idea. He's getting some sick pleasure out of watching Jordan suffer. I never meant to harm you and I am truly sorry for not taking you away when I had the chance. Then you wouldn't have to go through the things that Matt has planned. I do not have the power to stop him and frankly I'm a little too scared to try. I know you'll never love me like you love Jordan and I have accepted that but I couldn't let you die without knowing how I feel about you. I fell in love with you the first time I saw you in Sicily, but I know that I will never be the man you want. It's okay. Don't feel sad for me, after this is over I'll return to Sicily and eventually I'll find someone else but I'll never forget you. Never.

    Vincent

She didn't know if she wanted to cry or scream. Vincent had been here again, and he had not hurt her. But Matt would. He would hurt her just to further hinder Jordan. Macy was determined not to let that happen.

Jordan had already told her of his plan to go to Sandstone Garage with a police officer that would be dressed like her. He had contacted the officer who had originally investigated Matthew's alleged murder.

Everything was in place for tomorrow night. Macy was to stay at the house with Todd and Emma while an unmarked police car sat in front of the house. But Matthew wanted them both, and Macy knew that if they both didn't show up he would kill Jordan instantly and then come after her. She had to stop him. She knew that she and Jordan would never be safe until they were both behind bars.

If Vincent was watching her she could give him a sign. Lure him out and make him tell her where Matthew was. Macy went into the house and into the room she dreaded. She found a gun that she could hold in one hand comfortably and bullets right beside it. Just like Jordan to be so prepared. She slipped it into her sweat pants pocket and went to gather her purse. It was almost time for her meeting.

CHAPTER EIGHTEEN

The garage was located way beyond the city limits. It was, as expected, deserted and secluded, which meant that anything could happen and no one would know about it for at least a week or maybe even longer. This thought did not sit well with Jordan and he could tell that Diane, the officer who had been assigned to impersonate Macy, felt the same way.

"Are you ready?" She asked him as they sat in the car.

"As ready as I'll ever be," he said nervously. She checked her wire that had been taped to her chest and then she checked for the gun she had at her left ankle. Jordan didn't bother to tell her about the two pistols he had secured for his personal use. Matthew had a pretty good weapon on his side. Jordan knew this for a fact. He wasn't sure about Vincent's skill as a shooter or if he would even be there but he didn't want to leave anything to chance.

As they approached the building they noted that there were no other cars around. What if they didn't show up? Or what if it had been all just a set up and the building was rigged to explode upon entry? Jordan's mind replayed a million different scenarios.

"What do you think?" Diane asked.

"I'm not sure what to think." They both turned simultaneously as they heard an approaching vehicle. A black truck drove up and parked behind Jordan's car. The figure that got out of the front seat was Matthew. Jordan's throat went dry. For some reason he had been hoping that it was all just a tasteless joke and that Matthew had in fact been killed. But this man was his brother, of that Jordan was sure.

As he approached, Jordan glanced at Diane to convince himself that she looked enough like Macy to pull this off. She had Macy's build and her hair was dark brown, and although she didn't have the streaks of color in it like Macy's, they figured in the dark of night no one would be able to tell. Her eyes were also a dead giveaway; they weren't as soft as Macy's, but who would notice that besides Jordan?

Everything else looked enough like Macy he thought. He only hoped that Matthew wouldn't pay too much attention to her. After all it was Jordan that he truly wanted. Macy was just an innocent in this whole ordeal.

"I didn't think you'd bring her with you Jordan. What with the way you've kept her locked up since you returned. But I'm glad you had the good sense to do as I asked," Matthew stopped a few feet away from them, his pleasure evident in the evil grin that spread across his face.

"Why are you doing this Matt?" Jordan asked, barely restraining his anger.

"Let's not air our dirty laundry outside, Jordan. Shall we?" He walked past them and opened the door to the garage. After they had stood in the doorway for the first five minutes trying to figure out which way to go, Matthew switched on a light. There was a table and three chairs located in the corner, nothing else.

"Have a seat," Matthew said. They walked over to the table, Diane opting to sit further in the corner so that the light didn't shine so brightly on her.

"You're rather quiet tonight, Macy. Oh, can I call you Macy?" Matthew took off his jacket.

"That's fine but I'd like to get this over with so I can go home,"

Diane quipped, trying to sound like Macy.

"Well, I don't think that's going to happen tonight, so you might as well get comfortable." Matthew glared at her.

"I'd like to know why you're doing this when I've never done anything but love you."

"Come on man, how could you not know?" Matthew looked at his brother, disgust clear on his face. "Listen, I'll tell you what you need to know, when I think you need to know it. Right now I'm trying to get to know my future sister-in-law." Shifting his attention back to Macy, Matthew surveyed her once more.

This was the first time he had gotten a chance to see her close up. She was pretty, but nothing he'd fall for as hard as Jordan had. In fact, he thought she looked a little manly and wondered briefly if this was really Macy.

Deciding that Jordan wouldn't be stupid enough to mess with him at this stage of the game, Matthew continued to question her.

"So, when's my niece or nephew due to arrive?" Matthew asked Macy. "Don't look so shocked. I've known for some time now. Paris is a very good friend of mine. He keeps me informed of things like that." Matthew took note of Jordan's growing anger and it pleased him.

"My child will never call you uncle. You're not worthy of that title," Diane said smugly.

"Oh, well that's okay. You may change your mind later." There was a low knock at the door and Matthew got up to answer it. It was Paris.

"Where is he?" Matthew asked as he closed the door.

"I don't know, I looked all over for him. I even checked the airport in case he tried to skip town but he wasn't listed on any flights out today or tomorrow." Paris looked over at Jordan. Jordan silently prayed that he would not notice Diane. But he saw Paris' eyes move in her direction. He knew it wasn't Macy. What would he do now? Surprisingly he didn't say a word, he actually turned his back to him and faced Matthew giving him a complete run down of where he'd looked for Vincent.

"Fine. I'll deal with him later. Go get the ropes out of the truck. And don't forget the tape," Matthew ordered Paris. Paris never looked Jordan's way again.

"Did *your* brother turn on you too, Matt?" Jordan taunted.

"Shut up!! Your stupid-ass father is the only one who ever turned on anybody. That's why you're in this mess, so when you meet him in Hell remember to thank him!" Matthew was somewhat flustered. He was not pleased with Vincent's disappearance.

Jordan and Diane's hands were tied behind them and their ankles were likewise tied to the legs of the chair. As Paris tied his hands, Jordan noticed that the knot could have been tighter, a lot tighter and he took that as a sign of Paris' apology to him.

"Now, who wants to go first?" Matthew asked as he pulled out the Luger that he had stolen from Jordan's house.

Jordan's anger spiked as he recognized the weapon.

"You are sick. How can you do this to your brother? What has he done to you to make you behave like this?" Diane yelled, surprising Jordan as much as she did herself.

"Well, I guess you might as well know what you're dying for. It seems that our father has always regretted allowing his first wife to leave Sicily taking with her his two beloved sons. Even though, he didn't seem to have a problem requesting that she send the child she was carrying back to Sicily to be raised by him and his second wife as the heir to the Penelli fortune. You see, he could never love Santina, try as he did. She was not our mother. Santina, the lush, could not stand the insult that her marriage had become, so she told the child she had raised of his true heritage and of his brothers in the United States. Imagine my surprise when who should show up at my door one day but my long lost baby brother. He brought with him some interesting information," Matthew stated as he loaded the gun.

"Apparently, in his rage over her drunken manner, Dioncello had informed Santina that Vincent was not his heir. He had changed his will to reflect that his precious Theresa and his first-born son would be his rightful heirs in the event of his death. I figured that if Vincent and I forged a relationship with him, you know, developed some kind of father/son bond, he would change his mind and split the fortune between us instead." Checking to make sure the bullets were inserted correctly Matthew took the safety off the gun. "See, I knew that you despised the old man and would never reconcile with him, not even for money. So what was the point in you inheriting it? Besides you've got your own loot to spend. And Mother, well she was never interested in money anyway and I figured Penelli money would be more of a slap in the face for her to inherit. She only wanted the man, the man she couldn't have."

"So you decided that it was best to get us out of the picture so that you and Vincent would inherit it all," Jordan said disgustedly.

"Not exactly. At first, I thought that if we could just get him to change the will you and Mother would never have to know about it. I would move to Sicily and be content with my newfound riches. But after all of our efforts he still wouldn't change it. And to top it off he had contacted Mother and they were planning on reconciling," Matthew said looking amazed.

"You killed your own mother over money? I would have given you anything." Disbelief and pity echoed in Jordan's words. "Anything! I would have given you any amount you wanted. It wasn't necessary to kill her," his voice cracked.

"I didn't kill her." Matthew smirked. "What kind of person do you take me for? I couldn't do it myself and Vincent was chicken too, so Santina found a hitman and I paid him. I wasn't even in the country when it happened." Jordan remembered that Matthew hadn't attended the funeral. But now he knew why Dioncello had.

"After it was done, Dioncello took sick. The doctor said that it was only a matter of time before he died. Vincent and I knew that he wouldn't change the will now with Theresa gone so we decided that we needed to get you out of the picture also. It was my clever idea to fake my death so that in the end I wouldn't be fingered for anything. I'd be safe and sound in Sicily. I knew you'd be upset, but I didn't anticipate that you would come all the way to Sicily to see our father, the one person you hated most in this world. You thought he did it, didn't you?" Jordan was too stunned by what he was hearing to answer him. "Well, he didn't seem as upset about my death as I would have liked so I knew that it was now imperative to have you out of the way. But then you go and bring her into it." Matthew frowned and nodded towards Macy. "Silly Vincent has the hots for you, you know that don't you. And you like it, you're just like all the other teasers out there." Matthew glared angrily at Macy.

"If he hadn't kidnapped you this would have been taken care of by now. But that's okay, I'll take care of it tonight once and for all." Jordan saw Matthew raise the gun and point it at him, he had been trying to untie his hands during Matthew's story but he wasn't quite finished. He needed to reach his gun but there wasn't time. Matthew fired.

Jordan tried to fall to the floor before Matthew could get his shot off, but was late by a few seconds. The bullet ripped through the flesh in his left shoulder. The pain was blinding but he still fought to untie his hands. Just as he got them loose he looked up to see Matthew standing above him. Diane was screaming, unlike Macy who probably would have jumped out of her chair and lunged on Matthew by now. He heard a shot and saw Matthew open his mouth to scream; a scream that would never be heard.

His lifeless body hit the floor with a loud thump. Jordan untied his feet hastily and stared at the blood leaking from Matthew's temple. He looked around to see Paris standing at the far end of the garage holding a gun.

"I couldn't let him hurt you anymore, Jordan. I owe you that much," he said as he put the gun down. At that moment police officers came barging into the garage. Paris was handcuffed and taken away. After Diane was untied she went over to make sure Jordan was okay.

"You need to get to the hospital and get that checked out. You're losing a lot of blood," she said.

Jordan looked at his friend, one last time. He didn't know where he had gone wrong with Paris. And he had no idea why he thought he had to turn against him, but he couldn't deal with that now. "I need to call Macy first and let her know what's going on," he said moving towards his car. He dialed the number and waited for her to answer. He knew that she would be waiting by the phone so he was shocked when he didn't get any answer. Not even Joseph or Emma picked up. He didn't like the feeling he was getting. Diane saw the alarmed look in his eyes.

"What is it?" She asked.

"There's no answer. Nobody answered the phone. I have to get home." He jumped in the car and drove like a madman to get there.

CHAPTER NINETEEN

Macy's meeting had been productive. She had uncovered some things that shed a whole new light on this case, and she'd spotted Vincent peeking around the bushes in the back yard.

After eating a light lunch and talking Emma into letting her go outside by herself, Macy went in search of him. At first she didn't see him. She returned to the spot where she had seen him earlier and circled around the grounds twice. She feared he had left.

But as she turned to walk back to the back terrace he stepped from behind a potted plant where he knelt.

"Looking for someone?" He asked coyly.

"Shit!" Macy's hand went to her thumping heart. "You scared the hell out of me you idiot. Why didn't you just walk up to me like a normal person," she said struggling to catch her bearings.

"Why didn't you just call out to me instead of walking all around peeking behind bushes and flower beds?" He laughed. He still thought this was a game.

"What are you doing here?"

"I like seeing you. I like being near you." His hand was in her hair.

"Ringing the doorbell would be preferable the next time."

"Now you know that big brother of mine isn't about to let me come waltzing into his house. Besides I like to watch you, when you don't know I'm watching. It's more fun that way." His hand lingered on her cheek and came to rest on her shoulder. "I've missed you." His words were chilling to her. He believed that he loved her and he didn't see anything wrong with the things he was involved in. "Really?"

"Yup, I enjoyed our time in Sicily. I wish we could go back." His eyes roamed a little. "We were happy there. You could love me if we were there."

"Do you want to come in and sit down?" She wanted to get him in the house. Once in the house she knew that either Joseph or Todd would be able to subdue him.

"No. I just want to be with you," he said simply, in a child-like voice.

"What if you can't be with me?" She silently prayed that some-one would come looking for her and see him.

"I don't want to live if I can't be with you." He lowered his head and kissed her lightly on her cheek.

She didn't shudder and she didn't pull away. He was serious. He had feelings for her. And although she didn't share those feel-ings, she wasn't about to dismiss his without a care.

Out of the corner of her eye she saw Todd rounding the corner. He was quickly approaching them. She knew he would take Vincent down and a small part of her hurt for him and what he was about to go through.

"I love Jordan, Vincent. I could never love you the way I love him. I could have been your friend though.

"It doesn't matter anymore. After tonight it'll be all over. He'll never love you like I do!" And with that, Vincent felt Todd's strong arms come around his throat, as he was forcibly walked into the house.

Macy sighed for the life that was lost. "I hope to God he never loves me like you do," she said to herself.

Pulling into the driveway Jordan noticed that the lights were on and, the security system was still in tact. He dialed the code and proceeded up the driveway. Diane and two patrol cars pulled in behind him. As he got out of the car he heard them preparing to enter the house with him.

Forgetting the pain in his shoulders he fought against the fear that had clutched his heart. When he entered the house there was complete silence. The police officers split up and began a search. Jordan stood still trying to think of what could have happened. Vincent. Where was Vincent? Even though he was pretty sure Vincent would not hurt her, he was also sure that he had her. As he turned to leave the house and search the grounds he heard a noise coming from the closet. When he opened the door he saw Vincent tied up on the floor. His face bruised and bleeding he lay there gasping for air. The other officers hurried over to him quickly placing him in handcuffs.

"Where's Macy?" Were Jordan's only words to him.

"You don't deserve her, " Vincent said. Jordan grabbed him by the shirt and lifted him off the floor.

"What have you done to her? If she's hurt I swear I'll kill you!" Jordan said in a low growl.

"Would you now? Well, I'm sure where I'm going you'll have a difficult time pulling that off." Vincent smiled before a sick demented laughter overtook him.

"We'll find her Jordan, just give us a few minutes alone with him. You're too emotional right now. Why don't you let one of the officers take you to the hospital?" Diane asked.

"No, I have to find her." Jordan walked to the front door where the police had just escorted Vincent out of the house when he ran into a chest as broad as his own and stared into the face of his mirror image.

"Jordan. I must talk to you." Dioncello Penelli stood in the doorway flanked by two huge men that Jordan assumed were his bodyguards.

"Not now." Jordan couldn't deal with another thing tonight; he just needed to find Macy.

"No, now!" Dioncello roared. Jordan let out breath as his shoulders slumped. They walked into the kitchen and sat at the table.

"Are you alright?" Dioncello extended his hand to touch his son's wound.

"Yes! I'll be better once I find Macy." Jordan pulled away from him.

"She's fine." Dioncello said as he once again attempted to look at Jordan's shoulder. Jordan winced when he touched it. "You really should see a doctor son." He said.

"Where is she?"

"She's at my hotel with the rest of your staff."

"How did she get there?" Confused and getting dizzier by the minute Jordan struggled to keep from passing out.

"Well, it seems that you have one smart woman on your hands. When you returned from Sicily she sensed that there was some involvement with the firm she works for and your family so she checked it out. She didn't really get anywhere at first but then when the press got 'hold of the bodyguards and security systems, Max became concerned. He called me and said that I should come and check things out."

"Why would he call you? Do you know Maxwell Banks?" That was a stupid question; of course he had to know him.

"Maxwell Banks is the attorney I hired when your mother first brought you and your brother here. I wanted to keep an eye on all of you since I couldn't be with you physically. He's also married to my sister, AnaBella, which makes him your uncle. After your mother's death, I had him keep an even closer eye on the two of you. I knew there was something suspicious about her death, but I couldn't come up with anything. Then you turned up in New York. Max called me and asked if I had sent you there; I told him no, but to take care of you. And I see he did. Macy is a wonderful girl." Dioncello had grabbed some dishtowels that hung on a rack by the sink and used them to staunch the steady flow of blood coming from Jordan's shoulder.

"I don't understand. What does this have to do with Macy?" Jordan was dizzy and he was having trouble keeping all this information together.

"Well, you're the one who wanted her so you tell me? It seems that the Penelli men are attracted to the same types of women. Vincent was in love with her too; I presume you know that already." When Jordan didn't answer Dioncello continued. "He dropped off a letter to her yesterday, and she brought it to me. I decided that I needed to handle this situation and quickly."

"But how did you know that Vincent was here in the first place?"

"Santina. It seems my lovely wife had an attack of conscience and confessed some pretty shocking things to me a few weeks ago after Vincent escaped from prison. I knew they would come back to try again. But Macy didn't tell me about the letter Matthew had written to you until tonight. By that time I had already had the plan in place to get Vincent."

"What plan? Macy knew about this and didn't tell me?" Jordan asked. He was becoming lightheaded and the room spun around him.

"Macy knew that there was something else going on, and when Vincent sent her the letter she thought that she could use his feelings for her to get him to confess about what Matthew had done. Vincent followed Macy into town this morning and when she returned he was on the grounds waiting for her. That bodyguard saw him and detained Vincent until I could get here. I really didn't want the police involved so I told my men to keep him here until I could get here. It seems you arrived before me."

"Where are your men now?" Blood, thick and hot, seeped through Dioncello's fingers as he held the towel in place over Jordan's wound.

"You and the cops probably scared them away. I'm sure they're back at the hotel now."

"I want to see Macy now," Jordan said.

"No, I think you need to go to the hospital and I'll bring her to you." The dizziness was overwhelming and Jordan slid slowly from the chair. He figured he could trust Dioncello after everything that had happened. Besides he really didn't have much choice. He was out cold in the next instant.

CHAPTER TWENTY

Macy came through the door, the scent of vanilla breezily entering with her.

"Jordan, I was so worried about you. Your father said you had been shot, and I thought the worst. Oh, are you okay, baby?" Jordan pushed her away from him. Feeling supreme relief that she was in fact okay, but still very angry with her for not telling him everything that was going on.

"I thought I told you no secrets Macy," he said through clenched teeth.

"I know, but you would have been so angry if you knew that I had been in contact with your father."

"Stop calling him that." Jordan rolled his eyes.

"You really should give him a chance Jordan. He loves you, you know. As soon as he found out what Matthew and Vincent were planning to do, he came to stop them."

"If he had not sent us away it would have never happened. I would have had a normal childhood and my brothers would not have resented me. Now because of him I don't have any family. None, Macy, and you want me to forgive him," Jordan said finally.

"That's not true Jordan, you have me and our baby." Macy's hand went to her growing stomach. "And that, no matter how much you may hate to believe it, is because of him also. You are not a hurt child anymore. You're a grown man who is about to start his own family. Don't you think it's time you put the past to the side; it's the only way we can ever truly focus on the future."

"Macy, you know I would do anything for you." His hands joined hers at her mid-section. "But I don't know if I can forgive. You don't know what it was like watching my mother day after day, slowly dying because of his betrayal."

"But she was going to take him back. In the end, remember you told me that Matthew said they were going to reconcile. She was going to forgive him." Her hands cupped his face. "What do you think she would want you to do?"

"I don't know what to say." Conflict rose within him. He knew that what Macy was saying was right. If what Matthew had said were true, his mother was about to forgive his father and take him back. Had that happened he would have been faced with forgiving Dioncello years ago.

But now, so many things had changed. So many things had happened. And one of them was this beautiful woman that stood before him, carrying this little life that they had created together.

His child. He was having his own child. What type of example would he be if he had no forgiveness in his heart? He conceded that people were prone to make mistakes; he'd made quite a few in his short lifetime. And Dioncello had admitted his mistakes and was attempting to make them right.

Macy was right, it was time to put this hatred behind him and get on with his life. He had his own future to think of now and his family's. "What do I say? How do I even begin?"

"You don't have to say anything, son. I know that I have missed a lot over the years, and I cannot change the things that have happened. I just ask that you give me the chance to make things right now, give me a chance to see my grandchild grow up. That's all I ask." Jordan was shocked to see that Dioncello had been at the door, listening.

His shoulders slumped as part of the worry that had been weighing on him was lifted. It was time to move on. Like Dioncello had said, the past could not be changed.

Jordan's mind was still reeling from the events that had taken place. His brother, his confidant, had turned against him. His best friend had betrayed him. And a stranger that was linked to him by blood had kidnapped his woman. Could he possibly be having a nightmare, or maybe a bad dream that he would eventually awake from? He wished this were true.

But the fact of the matter was that he was lying in his bed recuperating from a gunshot wound inflicted by the brother he had grown up with. And the father he had hated all his life had actually cared about him, at least in his own twisted way.

Rage and pity battled inside of him. The realization that all the pain had stemmed from jealousy and money made it even more difficult to swallow. He had worked hard all his life to be successful and it hadn't earned him anything but grief, even though the fortune that had turned so many hearts hadn't been the one he had worked for, but rather the one that was his birthright.

Then there was Macy. He loved her more than he ever thought he'd love another human being. But after all he'd caused her to go through, he wouldn't blame her if she left. She had never wanted to come to L.A.; she had made that perfectly clear. But he'd forced her. He'd used his power and his money to get what he wanted. And now that same power and money wouldn't be enough to keep her should she decide to go.

These thoughts had plagued him night and day since he'd been in the hospital. But despair and fear had kept him quiet. Afraid that if he voiced his concerns they would become a reality; he held them inside and let them fester.

Now at home, Jordan was unusually quiet. He was taking a mild pain reliever but that wouldn't have made him the brooding specimen he'd been the last few days. Macy's attempts at talking to him or cheering him up had been futile. She was running out of ideas.

"Everything okay Ms. Macy?" Emma came into the kitchen where she was perched on a stool deep in thought.

"No, everything is not okay." Macy sighed. "Emma, I'm worried about Jordan. He seems so different now, so strange."

"I know what you mean. I was telling Joseph that very thing just yesterday." Emma took Macy's teacup and refilled it. "But you know, he's been through a lot these past few months."

"I guess you're right. I just wish there were a way I could reach him. If he talked about what was bothering him, I'm sure he'd feel better." Macy put lumps of sugar into her tea and stirred.

"Well, why don't you try and talk to him?"

"I have. He just pats my hand and tells me he's fine." Macy rolled her eyes, agitated by her own helplessness.

"Well, you're a smart woman Ms. Macy, and I hear you're a pretty good attorney." Emma told her.

"What does that have to do with anything?" Macy was slightly baffled at Emma's comment.

"I'm sure you've had a witness or two who haven't quite cooperated with you on the stand." Emma watched as Macy began to understand her meaning. "What do you do when they won't cooperate?"

"What I do to them usually gets me a threat to be held in contempt by the judge." Macy said thoughtfully. "But this isn't a courtroom so I have much more leeway here." Dropping the spoon into the cup she came off of the stool.

"Emma, we're eating in the dining room tonight." Macy walked to the entryway.

"You sure?"

"I'm positive."

Emma smiled at Macy's retreating back. "Watch out Mr. Jordan, here she comes."

CHAPTER TWENTY-ONE

Jordan absently flicked the channels not impressed by anything that was on the television. "Two hundred and twenty-two channels and there's not a damn thing on here to watch," he barked just as Macy came into the room.

"Then you won't mind if I turn it off." Not waiting for a reply Macy walked to the opposite side of the room and punched the power button. Moving over to the bed she pulled the sheets back, exposing Jordan's legs.

"What are you doing?" He reached for the covers that she held just out of his grasp.

"It's time for you to get up." Grabbing his feet she flung them over the side of the bed.

"I don't want to get up. I'm still recuperating you know." *What the hell was wrong with her?*

"Well I don't care what you want. You've been in this bed for two weeks. You were shot in the arm not in the butt. You can get out of bed." Macy stood with her hands on her hips. She couldn't pick him up; he'd have to cooperate in that regard. "Now get up and lets get you in the shower.

"I don't need a shower." He whined.

"The hell you don't."

"Macy what is your problem?" Grabbing her by the wrist he pulled her toward him.

"*I'm* not the one with the problem, Jordan. You are."

"Yeah! I've been shot if you don't recall."

"You were shot over three weeks ago. The doctor said you were healing fine. There's no reason for you to be holed up in this room anymore!" Macy screamed at him. "Unless, there's something you want to tell me." She let the words hang in the air.

"What would I have to tell you, Macy?"

"What's happened to you Jordan? What happened to the strong, possessive man I fell in love with?" She sat on the bed beside him, her wrists still in his hands.

"Is that what this is about? You miss me bossing you around." Jordan chuckled. "I thought you hated that."

"I did. I mean, I do. That's not what I'm talking about."

"Then what are you talking about Macy?"

"Something's changed. You've changed. You sit in this room all day and all night just playing with that stupid remote. I bring you your meals, or you get Emma to bring them to you and you just lie here. I don't understand. Is it me? Are you tired of me?" Macy's voice trembled and she willed back tears. *You're supposed to be interrogating him not whining like a baby*, she admonished herself.

"Is that what you think?" He spoke quietly, his grip on her wrists softening.

"I don't know what to think Jordan. All I know is something is wrong and I'd like to know what it is." Taking a chance she looked at him. Really looked at him. He was tired, his eyes were weary, and his shoulders slacked.

Jordan thought for a moment. Maybe he could tell her. Maybe she'd understand. He sure as hell didn't. He wanted to trust her. He wanted to trust that she'd be there, that she'd stay. But he'd trusted his brother. He'd trusted his friend.

But this was Macy. She said she loved him.

"I'm afraid Macy." He stared at the wall across the room, his body still as he waited for her to laugh. Surely the strong possessive man she fell in love with wouldn't be afraid of anything.

"Afraid of what?" Shifting slightly to face him she reached out and turned his face to hers. "What are you afraid of?"

Her eyes said he could trust her. She acted like she wanted to help. Jordan decided to take a chance.

"I'm afraid that you'll leave." He said simply. "After all that I've put you through, I'm afraid that you'll go back to New York."

His confession stunned her. Of all the things she'd thought could be bothering him, this had never crossed her mind. Just as the thought of leaving him and going back to New York hadn't crossed her mind.

"I thought you said this was my home."

"I did. But. . ."

"Well, why would I want to leave my home?"

"Macy I just don't know anymore. I thought I knew Matthew. I thought I knew that he was my brother and my friend. I thought I knew Paris and. . .

"And you thought that since they had betrayed you that I would do the same." She finished the sentence for him, a slight pain weighing on her heart. "How could you think that?"

Jordan looked away from her. "I don't know what to think anymore."

"I understand that your faith in people has been shaken. I certainly understand your hurt and confusion over what Paris and Matthew did to you. But what I don't understand is how you figured me to be like them."

"Not like them Macy. Just . . . just . . . well, you didn't want to come here in the first place." He defended himself.

"No, I didn't but you made me. You made me come here because you wanted me." Turning him to face her again she said,

"And I'm staying because I want *you*."

Her words warmed his heart. He stared into hazel eyes, those same hazel eyes he'd stared into that night at the ball. He loved her then, as he loved her now.

"I'm a jerk." He leaned his forehead on hers.

"Yup, a big silly jerk." She agreed with him.

"You still love me?"

"Unfortunately, I have a soft spot for big silly jerks." Smiling she kissed his upturned lips.

"Yeah, I just bet you do." Jordan pushed her back on the bed and continued kissing her.

It had been a month since that dreaded night and Macy was efficiently preparing for her first Christmas with Jordan. Vincent was safely tucked away behind bars, where he would most likely be for a long while.

Santina would not be leaving Sicily but she would suffer for her part in their plot, Dioncello promised to see to that. Jordan remained the primary heir to the Penelli fortune, until the birth of his first child, that is.

They were going to be married on New Year's Eve. Jordan would be finished with promotional shoots and appearances by then and they'd be able to take a nice honeymoon. Macy wanted to go back to Sicily, but Jordan wouldn't hear of it. They were going to Hawaii instead. Jordan's father had returned to Sicily last week after staying with them for a few weeks after Jordan had been released from the hospital. Macy had watched the two men try to make peace with each other. Their relationship was still pretty shaky, but Macy was glad to see that Jordan was at least giving it a try. He had even surprised her by inviting Dioncello to come back in the spring when the baby was due. She was very happy for them.

Maxwell Banks or Uncle Max, which he now insisted they call him, had come to L.A. to see Dioncello before he left. He wished Jordan and Macy much happiness and assured Macy that she would be a full-fledged partner on the first of the year.

It was funny, but the partnership that had meant so much to her in the past five years didn't have that big an impact on her now. She was actually toying with the idea of becoming an interior decorator instead. Jordan had only groaned when she'd suggested this to him.

She was content with her life and eager to become a mother, despite the circumstances. Her main concern now was building her new life with her husband and her child.

As she wrapped a present that she had bought for Emma she heard a lot of commotion in the downstairs hallway. She managed to get out of the chair without tipping over. She looked as though she were carrying twins but the doctor had assured her that it was only one baby, as she and Jordan had seen that last week on the sonogram; one very large baby.

She walked slowly down the steps taking care not to trip on the material of the flowing dress she wore. As she reached the bottom of the stairs she saw a small head with a short bobbed haircut on a woman no taller than she was. Tears sprang to her eyes.

"Mama, what are you doing here?" Eleanor Glenn turned to see her very beautiful, very pregnant daughter standing before her.

"My, my, have we gained weight?" Eleanor asked as she embraced Macy.

"I was going to call you."

"When? When you gave birth. If that man of yours hadn't called to tell me you were getting married, I would have missed that too. What's the matter with you child? Why didn't you tell me?" Eleanor scolded her eldest child.

"I don't know. I was waiting for the right time, but I guess I should have said something sooner."

"Maybe you should have. Then she wouldn't have dragged me across the country to make sure you were okay," Shena said from behind Eleanor. Macy hugged her sister who looked so much like her mother. While Macy had inherited her mother's thick hair, her complexion and her domineering personality had come from her father. Shena, on the other hand, was the spitting image of her mother. Right down to the soft-spoken voice and quiet brown eyes.

"Jordan called you?" Macy was astounded.

"He was worried about you spending the holidays away from your family, so he decided to bring your family here. I was wondering why you two just didn't come and visit but now I see why." She motioned to Macy's stomach.

"So when is my niece or nephew arriving?" Shena happily rubbed Macy's stomach.

"Some time around Easter. Come sit down and tell me everything that's been going on in New York," Macy said leading them to the family room.

"We'd much rather you tell us about all this murder and kidnapping we've read about." Although quiet, Eleanor had never been one to mince words.

Macy explained what had happened and then she listened to Shena talk about school and men. They visited for three hours lounging on the couch. And that's how Jordan found them when he came home.

"A man could do worse than to come home to a room full of beautiful women," he said smiling.

"He looks even better in person. Way to go Sis," Shena whispered as she nudged Macy.

"Jordan, this is my mother Eleanor and my sister Shena," Macy said stumbling out of the chair.

"I know, *Bella*." He helped her out of the chair and kissed her cheek. "How are we today?" Placing a hand on her stomach in greeting to his growing child.

"We're just fine. Actually we're great now that I'll be able to share Christmas with all the people I love." Kissing him again, Macy beamed with happiness.

CHAPTER TWENTY-TWO

Macy wore a Vera Wang original maternity wedding gown. The smooth ivory satin molded against her growing girth and the simple pillbox hat boasted a pearl-trimmed veil. Jordan's ivory suit hung expertly on his broad shoulders; the ice blue tie glistened at his collar.

Eleanor had given her eldest daughter away while Shena stood by her side as her maid of honor. Dioncello and Maxwell Banks stood at Jordan's side. And as the justice of the peace pronounced them man and wife the clock struck twelve, and they began the New Year as husband and wife.

On the first day of spring in a birthing room at the Beverly Medical Center, Sasha Dioncella Blake came into the world with a wailing cry. Her father, who had been momentarily speechless, watched her contented now.

"She is almost as beautiful as her mother." Jordan held his daughter in his arms.

"I think she looks just like her father."

"Well, I personally think she favors her grandfather." Dioncello said with his chest poked out. He was the paragon of a proud grandparent.

"Well, she'll be spoiled rotten that's for sure," Eleanor said as she eyed the two men. "But she is a darling little one isn't she."

Jordan leaned over and kissed Macy. *"Come sei Bella. Ti adoro, angelo mio."* He whispered in her ear. She had finally found out what it meant, and it warmed her to her toes every time he said it.

AUTHOR BIOGRAPHY

Artist C. Arthur was born and raised in Baltimore, Maryland where she currently resides with her husband and three children. She has worked in the legal field for thirteen years as first, a secretary, then receiving a degree in paralegal studies. She has encompassed every area of law and is now primarily in defense litigation.

An active imagination and a love for reading encouraged her to begin writing in high school and she hasn't stopped since. With the preferred genre of romance/mainstream her ultimate goal is to create entertaining and informative characters, bringing to life a range of social, economic and health issues.

A LARK ON THE WING
BY PHYLISS HAMILTON
SEPTEMBER 2003

CHAPTER ONE

"For crying our loud, of all days for it to rain!" Thoroughly exasperated at both the weather and the course that her carefully planned day was taking, Sedona quickly changed lanes as she seized an opportunity to maneuver her convertible forward. One thing that could be said about New Orleans rush-hour traffic, with or without the rain, was that its pace aptly matched the city's famous moniker, "The Big Easy." *C'mon girlfriend, keep your cool,* she admonished herself. *While everyone else is driving as if it's Sunday in the park, your blood pressure is spinning triple digits.* After riding the bumper of the car ahead of hers for several blocks, Sedona nudged into an opening and finally broke free of the pack. If luck was on her side, she could just make the traffic light that was preparing to change its green arrow to yellow. Ten good seconds that was all that she needed. Despite the fact that there were rail tracks crossing the intersection, she was determined to take it all the way. Just as she floored the accelerator, a city utility truck positioned further down in the adjacent lane, decided that he too wanted to make the arrow and jumped ahead of her. *Okay, don't despair, if we both hurry, the arrow is still ours for the taking. Come on truck — no guts, no glory. Pick up speed . . . c'mon . . . make the turn . . . make . . .* Never had she slammed on her brakes so hard.

"You . . . you . . . idiot! Why didn't you make the turn?"

The truck driver, thoroughly oblivious to the fact that he foiled her strategy, returned her scowl with a broad grin via his rear view mirror. Never had she wanted to wipe a smile off of a man's face so badly. Taking a deep breath, she momentarily closed her eyes to regain control of her temper. *Get a grip, Sedona. That man is not even thinking about you, and you're allowing yourself to go off the deep end. Where's your control? Control belongs to you . . . remem - ber promise #4.* Good Lord, when was the last time that she pulled that one out? It seemed like another lifetime ago, seven years to be exact, when the therapist encouraged her to write a contract to herself centered on a set of promises. At the time, her first thought was that she was being handed a load of 'psycho-babble' manure. The only promises that she was interested in making were that she would never again be so feeble-minded and desperate for love and affection as to fall head over heels *in* love. In fact, she was determined that the next time that a man came knocking at her heart, the blinders would be off, her radar calibrated, and the 'proceed with caution'flag up and waving high. Humph. . . she must have *inhaled* and *exhaled* at least a half a dozen times since then, and now here she was again, back to reciting promises about control.

Ding . . . ding . . . ding! *Control my ass, I don't believe it! A train, a freakin' train. It would have to be today of all days.* Helplessly watching the railroad-crossing gate descend, she angrily banged the steering wheel when the truck driver ahead of her, ignored the flashing red lights and raced across the tracks. *He has the courage to beat a train, but couldn't make a turn on yellow.* Exasperated, she brought back her head heavily against the seat as she took in the sluggish speed of the train. With no end in sight, it was obvious that she would be stuck waiting for a very long time. *The story of my life.*

Sedona, determined to make the best of her lot, turned off the dashboard clock — no point of blaring reminders — and reached for her favorite CD. Maybe a little Lou Rawls would help to 'destress,' she reasoned. So, with attention shifted from the ambling train to the music carrel, she flipped through an eclectic collection of about twenty albums. After searching through the music several times, she felt her fuse reignite. *C'mon I just played the darn thing the other day.* Remembering that she had taken the CD into the house the evening before to play while she e-mailed her *friend,* Austin, she dropped her head back against the seat at the thought of him waiting for her at the airport. *Austin, baby, I'm sorry. I know that you must be indubitably fuming by now.* "Indubitably," repeated Sedona aloud. In fact, fuming would be putting it mildly. Austin had little patience for triflers — those who couldn't manage time, money, and/or emotions.

At the beginning, she assumed that Austin James' pragmatic take on life had to do more with his years as a physician in the Navy than anything else. But as she had gotten to know him, she had come to the conclusion that in all likelihood, he had stepped out of his mother's womb focused and ready to do battle with life. In fact, his layette probably included a wristwatch, day-planner, and the map of his life with all of its various paths and side trips marked out and brightly highlighted. Austin was about as military as they came — punctual, efficient, forever practical and at times, infuriatingly self-possessed. He was one of those people who without much effort, were always prepared, always correct, always . . . well just always whatever they are supposed to be, should be, or aspiring to be at the time.

Ordinarily 'perfect' people irritated her, they tended to be not only smug in their certainty of having gotten 'it'right, but they were also a constant reminder of her own imperfections. Until her divorce seven years before, her life seemed to be comprised of nothing but 'perfect'people. Both her parents and ex-husband were long standing members of the 'perfect'set. But Austin, 'emotionally detached'though he was, seldom made her free-spirit style seem less than acceptable. In fact, his amused appreciation of her spontaneity and colorful expressions validated what her mother often referred to as her 'attitude.' On the prerequisite flip side though, despite his seeming acceptance, she was never quite sure as to how Austin interpreted their friendship or level of commitment. She had learned from her ex-husband to make no assumptions concerning how committed a man is to a relationship. Hell, usually it isn't even *'how'* committed, but *'if'* he's committed.

With the train's end still nowhere in sight, she passed the time by touching up her makeup. Between God blessing her with clear skin and good looks, and her mother teaching her how to properly care for and protect her face from the unrelenting sun, she needed very little to enhance her natural beauty. From the satiny nutmeg complexion given to her by her mother, to the thick coarse hair gifted by her dad, she was an attractive composite of all of the pluses that her gene pool had to offer. For years, the one gene that she used to wish that she could have waved aside with a "thank you, but no" was the low-resonating timbre of her voice. Often mistaken over the phone as her mother's growing up, she used to try to raise its pitch a notch of two by adding a bit of perkiness. As an adult though, having come to terms with the fact that despite her efforts to the contrary she would always possess tones of her mother, she tried to view the similarities as positives, and in some cases, even as her strengths.

Soft and sexy, that was her aim for the evening. Usually, she allowed her natural bent for the practical to rule her style of dress, another trait inherited from her mother, but not tonight. With muted fuchsia as her palate, she dispensed with the classic clean lines that filled her closet, and instead wrapped her Nubian thighs, breasts, and hips in a sinfully sensuous silk. Not quite the way Austin last saw her, that's for sure.

As Lou Rawls seductively stated his case, ". . . Cause I know what you want, yes I know what you need," Sedona sang in agreement, "Let me be good to you." Almost as if on cue, the train's caboose passed and the crossing gates lifted. Gunning across the tracks, Sedona turned the corner and broke free of the pack as her mind turned to her very first encounter with Dr. Austin James. . . . *to be continued.. .*

For more, pick up this title online at www.genesis-press.com or at you local bookstore in September.

2003 Publication Schedule

January	Twist of Fate	Ebony Butterfly II
	Beverly Clark	Delilah Dawson
	1-58571-084-9	1-58571-086-5
February	Fragment in the Sand	Fate
	Annetta P. Lee	Pamela Leigh Starr
	1-58571-097-0	1-58571-115-2
March	One Day At A Time	Unbreak my Heart
	Bella McFarland	Dar Tomlinson
	1-58571-099-7	1-58571-101-2
April	At Last	Brown Sugar Diaries & Other Sexy Tales
	Lisa G. Riley	Delores Bundy & Cole Riley
	1-58571-093-8	1-58571-091-1
May	Three Wishes	Acquisitions
	Seressia Glass	Kimberley White
	1-58571-092-X	1-58571-095-4
June	When Dreams A Float	Revelations
	Dorothy Elizabeth Love	Cheris F. Hodges
	1-58571-104-7	1-58571-085-7
July	The Color of Trouble	Someone To Love
	Dyanne Davis	Alicia Wiggins
	1-58571-096-2	1-58571-098-9
August	Object Of His Desire	Hart & Soul
	A. C. Arthur	Angie Daniels
	1-58571-094-6	1-58571-087-3
September	Erotic Anthology	A Lark on the Wing
	Assorted	Phyliss Hamilton
	1-58571-113-6	1-58571-105-5

October	Angel's Paradise	I'll be your Shelter
	Janice Angelique	Giselle Carmichael
	1-58571-107-1	1-58571-108-X
November	A Dangerous Obsession	Just An Affair
	J.M. Jeffries	Eugenia O'Neal
	1-58571-109-8	1-58571-111-X
December	Shades of Brown	By Design
	Denise Becker	Barbara Keaton
	1-58571-110-1	1-58571-088-1

Other Genesis Press, Inc. Titles

A Dangerous Deception	J.M. Jeffries	$8.95
A Dangerous Love	J.M. Jeffries	$8.95
After the Vows	Leslie Esdaile	$10.95
(Summer Anthology)	T.T. Henderson	
	Jacqueline Thomas	
Again My Love	Kayla Perrin	$10.95
Against the Wind	Gwynne Forster	$8.95
A Lighter Shade of Brown	Vicki Andrews	$8.95
All I Ask	Barbara Keaton	$8.95
A Love to Cherish	Beverly Clark	$8.95
Ambrosia	T.T. Henderson	$8.95
And Then Came You	Dorothy Elizabeth Love	$8.95
A Risk of Rain	Dar Tomlinson	$8.95
Best of Friends	Natalie Dunbar	$8.95
Bound by Love	Beverly Clark	$8.95
Breeze	Robin Hampton Allen	$10.95
Cajun Heat	Charlene Berry	$8.95
Careless Whispers	Rochelle Alers	$8.95
Caught in a Trap	Andre Michelle	$8.95
Chances	Pamela Leigh Starr	$8.95
Dark Embrace	Crystal Wilson Harris	$8.95
Dark Storm Rising	Chinelu Moore	$10.95
Designer Passion	Dar Tomlinson	$8.95
Eve's Prescription	Edwina Martin Arnold	$8.95
Everlastin' Love	Gay G. Gunn	$8.95
Fate	Pamela Leigh Starr	$8.95
Forbidden Quest	Dar Tomlinson	$10.95
From the Ashes	Kathleen Suzanne	$8.95
	Jeanne Sumerix	
Gentle Yearning	Rochelle Alers	$10.95

Glory of Love	Sinclair LeBeau	$10.95
Heartbeat	Stephanie Bedwell-Grime	$8.95
Illusions	Pamela Leigh Starr	$8.95
Indiscretions	Donna Hill	$8.95
Interlude	Donna Hill	$8.95
Intimate Intentions	Angie Daniels	$8.95
Kiss or Keep	Debra Phillips	$8.95
Love Always	Mildred E. Riley	$10.95
Love Unveiled	Gloria Greene	$10.95
Love's Deception	Charlene Berry	$10.95
Mae's Promise	Melody Walcott	$8.95
Meant to Be	Jeanne Sumerix	$8.95
Midnight Clear (Anthology)	Leslie Esdaile Gwynne Forster Carmen Green Monica Jackson	$10.95
Midnight Magic	Gwynne Forster	$8.95
Midnight Peril	Vicki Andrews	$10.95
My Buffalo Soldier	Barbara B. K. Reeves	$8.95
Naked Soul	Gwynne Forster	$8.95
No Regrets	Mildred E. Riley	$8.95
Nowhere to Run	Gay G. Gunn	$10.95
Passion	T.T. Henderson	$10.95
Past Promises	Jahmel West	$8.95
Path of Fire	T.T. Henderson	$8.95
Picture Perfect	Reon Carter	$8.95
Pride & Joi	Gay G. Gunn	$8.95
Quiet Storm	Donna Hill	$8.95
Reckless Surrender	Rochelle Alers	$8.95
Rendezvous with Fate	Jeanne Sumerix	$8.95
Rivers of the Soul	Leslie Esdaile	$8.95

Rooms of the Heart	Donna Hill	$8.95
Shades of Desire	Monica White	$8.95
Sin	Crystal Rhodes	$8.95
So Amazing	Sinclair LeBeau	$8.95
Somebody's Someone	Sinclair LeBeau	$8.95
Soul to Soul	Donna Hill	$8.95
Still Waters Run Deep	Leslie Esdaile	$8.95
Subtle Secrets	Wanda Y. Thomas	$8.95
Sweet Tomorrows	Kimberly White	$8.95
The Price of Love	Sinclair LeBeau	$8.95
The Reluctant Captive	Joyce Jackson	$8.95
The Missing Link	Charlyne Dickerson	$8.95
Tomorrow's Promise	Leslie Esdaile	$8.95
Truly Inseperable	Wanda Y. Thomas	$8.95
Unconditional Love	Alicia Wiggins	$8.95
Whispers in the Night	Dorothy Elizabeth Love	$8.95
Whispers in the Sand	LaFlorya Gauthier	$10.95
Yesterday is Gone	Beverly Clark	$8.95
Yesterday's Dreams, Tomorrow's Promises	Reon Laudat	$8.95
Your Precious Love	Sinclair LeBeau	$8.95

ESCAPE WITH INDIGO !!!!

Join Indigo Book Club©
It's simple, easy and secure.

Sign up and receive the new releases
every month + Free shipping and
20% off the cover price.

Go online to www.genesis-press.com
and click on Bookclub or
call 1-888-INDIGO-1

Subscribe Today
to
Blackboard Times

The African-American
Entertainment Magazine

Get the latest in book reviews, author interviews, book ranking,

hottest and latest tv shows, theater listing and more . . .

Coming in September

blackboardtimes.com

Order Form

Mail to: Genesis Press, Inc.

1213 Hwy 45 N
Columbus, MS 39705

Name _____

Address _____

City/State _____ Zip _____

Telephone _____

Ship to (if different from above)

Name _____

Address _____

City/State _____ Zip _____

Telephone _____

Qty.	Author	Title	Price	Total

Use this order form, or call 1-888-INDIGO-1	**Total for books** _____ **Shipping and handling:** **$5 first two books, $1 each additional book** **Total S & H** _____ **Total amount enclosed** _____ *Mississippi residents add 7% sales tax*